"Last-minute panic isn't uncommon at weddings."

Sean's eyes coaxed her. "A pity you didn't come out with all this weeks ago. Now we have only an hour. You can't leave me standing at the altar."

"Can't I?"

Miranda got out of the car, and her father hurried forward. His eyes were brilliant with anxiety and distress. "The wedding is still on, then?" He looked at Miranda, but it was Sean who answered.

"It's going ahead as planned."

Her father gave a sigh, and Miranda saw the relief in his face. Sean was right. It was too late to back out of the wedding now. But she didn't know how she was going to cope with being Sean's wife while he did not love her.

The panic her father and Sean had felt might be over, but hers had just begun.

CHARLOTTE LAMB began to write "because it was one job I could do without having to leave the children. At the start my writing was very much a hobby." Now writing is her profession. She has had more than forty Harlequin novels published since she began writing in 1978. "I love to write," she explains, "and it comes very easily to me." Once she begins a story, the plot, the actions and personalities of her characters develop almost spontaneously. She and her family live in a beautiful old home on the Isle of Man, between England and Ireland. Charlotte spends eight hours a day working at her typewriter—and she enjoys every minute of it.

Books by Charlotte Lamb

HARLEQUIN PRESENTS
842—WHO'S BEEN SLEEPING IN MY BED?
851—SLEEPING DESIRE
874—THE BRIDE SAID NO

HARLEQUIN ROMANCE
2181—MASTER OF COMUS
2206—DESERT BARBARIAN
2696—KINGFISHER MORNING

These books may be available at your local bookseller.

Don't miss any of our special offers. Write to us at the following address for information on our newest releases.

Harlequin Reader Service
901 Fuhrmann Blvd.
P.O. Box 1325, Buffalo, NY 14269
Canadian address: P.O. Box 2800, Postal Station A,
5170 Yonge St., Willowdale, Ont. M2N 6J3

CHARLOTTE LAMB

the bride said no

Harlequin Books

TORONTO • NEW YORK • LONDON
AMSTERDAM • PARIS • SYDNEY • HAMBURG
STOCKHOLM • ATHENS • TOKYO • MILAN

Harlequin Presents first edition April 1986
ISBN 0-373-10874-5

Original hardcover edition published in 1985
by Mills & Boon Limited

CHAPTER ONE

MIRANDA dived into the library and was relieved to find it empty, just one table lamp lit and the long room otherwise plunged into shadow. She needed to be alone, even if only for five minutes; she had been talking to people for what seemed days and her face had set into an unreal, unconvincing mask, her smile stiff, her jaws aching, her temples throbbing. She walked across the deep-piled carpet, kicking off her shoes; even her feet hurt from hours of standing around on the delicate high heels. Why had she given in to her father's insistence on a huge family party tonight? Heaven only knew what time she would get to bed and she would have liked an early night. Tomorrow was going to be a long day.

She stood in front of a gilt-framed mirror on one shadowy wall and stared at herself. Her face seemed unfamiliar. Was that really her? She didn't recognise herself; her dark blue eyes had the deep burning glow of fatigue and boredom and her skin was feverishly flushed.

'Tomorrow,' she said aloud, her voice unsteady, and felt her skin grow so hot that she put her hands to her cheeks, laughing shakily. Where was Sean tonight? What was he doing? Drinking with his friends in some nightclub? She had teased him about it that morning.

'Planning an all-night stag party?'

'A wake?' he had mocked back, his dark eyes gleaming down at her. 'It's an idea—any objections?'

'Not as long as you don't have a hangover tomorrow, and forget to turn up at the church!'

'Oh, I'll be there, don't worry,' he had said in that deep, husky voice which always made her stomach clench with fierce excitement, and then he had bent and kissed her, and the mere memory of that kiss made her breathing quicken. At times Miranda was almost frightened by the depth of her love for him. It wasn't the physical side of love that alarmed her—on the contrary, that made her veins run with fever every time she thought about the nights to come. Miranda was afraid of her own vulnerability where Sean was concerned, she was afraid she loved him too much, more than he loved her, and whenever she thought about that she had a premonition of pain.

She turned away from the too-revealing mirror with a frown and wandered over to the floor-length red velvet curtains that masked the windows. Slipping behind them she leaned her hot face on the glass, sighing at the coolness of it on her skin. The night sky was virtually clear, a horned silver moon drifted through what clouds there were and shone through the edges of them, giving them a blurred silvery radiance. Frost stiffened the grass on the immaculate lawns, the skeletal trees were silhouetted around the edges of the garden.

Miranda was about to go back into the room

when she heard the library door open and a low voice which she recognised with a frown.

'Nobody in here, thank God.'

Miranda stood very still, hardly breathing, hoping that the new arrivals would go out, but although the door clicked shut again the voices were louder, their owners were in the room with her.

'Collection of dead bores, I thought I was going to scream if I didn't get away but if Ferdy saw me slipping off before everyone else, he'd kick up merry hell next time he saw me. When you work for him, he owns you body and soul.' The woman's voice had a purring, feline tone; Miranda heard it with a prickle of distaste but no real surprise. She had never heard her father's secretary talk about him in that particular tone before, but it came as no shock to her that Diana Cobbold could be malicious, even if she had always been careful to sheath her claws behind silken pads when Ferdy was around. Diana was a tall, curvy blonde with slanty green eyes. However sweetly she smiled, those cat's eyes gave her away.

'I've often wondered about that,' the man said and Miranda listened intently, trying to pinpoint the face to which this voice belonged. She had talked to him earlier, she was sure of it—but who was he?

'Finish that whisky, darling—there's a decanter of his vintage port in here. Where is it?' Miranda heard the silken swish of Diana's skirts and a little exclamation of satisfaction. 'Ah, here it is on this table—a bottle of this stuff sets him back as much as you earn in commission for a week, Paul.'

The man gave a low whistle. 'He can afford it. I'd like to know what that girl will be getting for a wedding settlement.'

Diana laughed and Miranda heard her pouring something into a glass, then the click with which she dropped the crystal stopper back into the decanter.

'She'll get Sean Hinton—it's Sean who'll be getting the settlement. I heard him discussing it with Ferdy months ago. Once he's married her, Sean gets the managing director's chair and a fat block of family shares. No fool, our Sean! Before he proposed he checked with Daddy to make sure he would get what he wanted. It makes me sick to hear all those hypocrites out there talking as if this was a romantic love match when they all know Ferdy bought Sean for her. As I said, when you work for Ferdy, he owns you body and soul.'

Miranda had almost burst through the smothering velvet curtains while Diana was talking, but she bit down on her lower lip to stifle the angry cry which tried to escape. She couldn't bear to hear what Diana was saying—it wasn't true, she didn't believe a word of it, but it made her feel sick. Even less could she bear the thought of Diana knowing that she had overheard her vicious lies, so she stood very still, her body taut with shock, as stiff as the icy grass out there under the moon.

'Does he own *you*, darling?' the man asked and

the insinuation in his voice made Miranda's face quiver with cold disgust.

'He thinks he does,' Diana said.

'*Body* and soul?' The man laughed. 'That was what you said, wasn't it?'

'That's what he wants—but I'm not that stupid. I wouldn't be the first, no doubt, but he never married any of the others, and if I have my way I'll make damn certain I'm the last. Once the girl is married he'll start seeing it my way.'

'You're very sure of yourself.' The man sounded admiring. Miranda could easily picture Diana as she talked; the other woman had a perfectly proportioned face which might have been beautiful if not for that touch of felinity, the slant of the deepset green eyes, the faint shortening of the nose, something spiteful in the curve of the mouth which Diana invariably painted a glossy pink.

'I have his number,' Diana said with triumph. 'He's vain, that's his weakness. He doesn't want to believe he's nearly sixty; to have a wife half his age will boost his ego.'

'But you said yourself that he'd never married any of the others.' It was easy to see why Diana was so confiding with this unseen man; he had her sort of character, his purring voice was full of mocking malice. 'I don't doubt he fancies you, anyone with half an eye could see that, but you may have bitten off more than you can chew when you try to get a proposal out of him.'

'Do you know why he never married any of the others?' Diana asked, walking away across the room, her voice less audible the further she got from the window. 'He made some ludicrous promise to his wife, when she was dying—she was scared that he'd marry the wrong sort of woman, someone who wouldn't be kind to her precious Miranda—so she got Ferdy to promise her that he wouldn't marry again until Miranda got married. Cunning of her, wasn't it? Miranda was only twelve when her mother died. Ten years without a wife—oh, yes, Ferdy will be ripe for picking once the girl has gone, and if I have a son we'll see how much of the company Sean Hinton gets.'

'My God, there are brains behind those green eyes,' the man said, laughing. 'I hope you pull it off, darling, and don't forget that blood is thicker than water. I'm tired of living on commission, I wouldn't say no to a good desk job with prospects.'

'Don't worry, Paul, I won't forget you. I'm going to need allies if I'm going to fight Sean Hinton.'

'This calls for a celebration—I'll have another glass of that port, it's terrific stuff, old Ferdy knows port, I'll say that for him.'

'No, he'll be wondering where I've got to—we mustn't stay in here any longer, Paul.' The door opened. 'I'll go now, stay here for a few minutes and slip out when the coast is clear.'

Miranda heard the man blow a kiss, laughing, then the door closed quietly and she heard the man walk back towards her. She froze, her face as white as the frost on the window pane, then heard him pouring himself some more port. He drank it audibly, then after a moment while he whistled and prowled around the room, he went out as softly as Diana had done, and Miranda leaned back, trembling.

She felt unclean, as though she had woken up from some happy dream to find a snake crawling over her face. It wasn't true, any of it. Of course she knew that, but hearing Diana's soft voice saying such things about her father, about her, about Sean, made her feel ill. The snake's poison fangs had bitten too suddenly, too deeply; the poison was circulating in her blood. Sean loved her, it wouldn't have mattered to him if she hadn't had a penny to her name. Diana was lying when she said that Sean and her father had bargained over her before Sean proposed, as though she was a company to be disposed of, her assets calculated, her price fixed. It was a lie, she didn't even need to think about it to be sure of that.

Sean was going to become managing director after their marriage, that was true, but that had nothing to do with her. Her father had intended to make him managing director anyway. Ferdy had told her that he found it too gruelling to run the day to day affairs of the company, he was kicking himself upstairs, becoming chairman and leaving what he called 'the dull stuff' to Sean.

Diana had taken a truth and twisted it to build a lie. Miranda had always known that Diana didn't like her—it had been on the periphery of her awareness whenever she was in the same room as her father's secretary, but she had never taken much notice of the other woman's hostility because it hadn't really mattered what Diana thought of her. Diana was just one more in the long line of her father's secretaries, who had come and gone every few years without Miranda taking any notice of them. Looking back, though, she realised how attractive they had all been, and a frown jerked her brows together. Had there been one small grain of truth in what Diana had said?

She winced, pushing her way through the clinging folds of velvet curtain. The room seemed suddenly different, she looked around it with distaste. It would always be the place where she had heard a soft voice saying malicious, wounding things about her and the two men she loved. The shadows seemed thicker, the blood red of the leather on her father's desk had an ominous hue, the gilding on the spines of books lining the walls glittered menacingly. Her father liked his wealth to be visible; he had spared no expense in furnishing his home. Ferdy had built up a successful company, but he had been poor as a child and he needed to see tangible proof that he no longer needed to worry over where the next meal was coming from. Miranda had always been touched by his almost childlike delight in his own achievements. That made him more human, and Ferdy was quite daunting if one merely looked at what he had built, the great company whose profits increased every year, the wealth he had amassed. The autocratic, ruthless man who had succeeded in the face of overwhelming odds was not as easy to love as the Ferdy who exulted happily over his expensive possessions while he looked back in wonder at the poverty of his childhood.

Diana had shown her a new vision of her father, and Miranda shivered, remembering what the other woman had said. It hadn't even occurred to her that her father might be having affairs, she hadn't ever seen her father in such a light. She felt a fool as she realised in what a simple, limited way she had thought about Ferdy. He was her father and she loved him, and that was the sum total of her vision of Ferdy. She had been naïve.

A cold little voice inside her head asked: if you were naïve about Ferdy, how sure are you about Sean?

She turned hurriedly away, refusing even to listen. She wanted to get out of this room, she must forget she ever heard that conversation, she wished to God she had come out from behind the curtains before Diana and her companion started talking. She was almost at the library door before she realised her feet were bare. Halting, she looked around for her shoes, remembering that she had kicked them off when she first came into the room.

They were lying under her father's desk; she had to kneel down to reach them. As she began to get up she crashed her head into the solid edge of the table and tears sprang into her eyes. She crouched there, clutching her forehead with one hand and her shoes with the other.

'Damn, damn, damn.'

Shakily getting up, she went over to look into the mirror. Her face was white and drawn now; she ached as she remembered how it had looked a quarter of an hour ago when it wore the hectic flush of excitement, the sensual glitter of expectation. Where had that look gone? Diana had erased it with a few malicious, lying words.

What was she going to do about Diana? she thought, gingerly touching the bump on her temples and wincing. How was she going to explain the bruise away? She was so cold; shock was exhausting. She trod into her shoes and turned away from the mocking mirror. Should she tell her father what she had overheard? She couldn't. She could not repeat any of that, it would make her sick.

Do you really think he would tell you if it *was* the truth? asked that still cold voice inside her head.

It isn't true, any of it, she protested, walking unsteadily to the door, but she knew she wouldn't be able to bring herself to ask her father any questions, she was too afraid of the answers she might get. Yet how could she go ahead with her marriage to Sean when her head was full of buzzing, unanswered questions? She was so confused that she wasn't even sure exactly what questions she needed to ask. How much of Diana's remarks had some core of truth? Had Ferdy had affairs with some of his other secretaries? Had he promised Sean that if he married Miranda, he would get the company? As soon as she had formed that question in her mind she bit her lip, denying that it could be true, knowing that she wouldn't ever ask her father such a thing. That didn't wipe out the hovering question mark in her mind, though, did it? That was the real danger of half-lies—they were half-truths as well, and Diana had sown her seeds of doubt cleverly. Miranda might try to reject them but she already felt them sprouting inside her head.

Once she was outside the library she could hear the noise of the party which the massive library door had excluded; people were wandering from room to room, drinks in their hands, behind their voices the throb of music from the stereo in the drawing-room. Miranda hovered, watching a group of her relatives talking, wishing she dared sneak upstairs and go to bed, but knowing that if she did, her father would come up in search of her.

'Hi, Miranda, getting cold feet yet?'

She turned with a start and forced a smile when she recognised one of her young cousins. 'Oh, hallo, Polly.'

'You're looking tired.' Polly Stansfield's brown eyes widened as they stared. 'Hey, what have you done to your head? That's a nasty looking bump. Don't tell me Sean's started beating you up already?'

Miranda put a hand to her forehead, trying to look cheerful. 'I dropped something and when I bent to pick it up I banged my head on a table. Does it look as big as it feels?'

'You ought to put a cold compress on it or something, or you're going to have a big bruise there tomorrow.' Polly put a hand under her arm. 'Look, come into the bathroom and I'll see what I can do.' She was a level-headed, energetic girl, a year younger than Miranda and worked as a secretary in a hospital which presumably gave her a sketchy idea of how to cope in a medical emergency. She had been rather bossy as a child and that aspect of her character hadn't diminished as she grew older. Her mother was Miranda's mother's sister; the Stansfields had little money but Miranda had often envied her cousins, in the way an only child does envy other children who come from a large family. Aunt Ann had six children; their house was noisy and crowded and full of fun.

As they went upstairs they kept passing people who smiled at Miranda and said things like: 'Only twelve hours to D-Day!' or 'Having a good time?' One or two stared and said: 'Who won the fight?' and looked curiously at her bruised, wan face.

'Is something wrong?' Polly asked, gently holding a cold flannel to her forehead in the bathroom.

'I've got a headache now, that's all,' Miranda lied.

Polly glanced down probingly but didn't press her. 'I love your dress,' she said instead and Miranda managed to smile.

'Thank you.'

'I used to get a lot of your clothes, remember?

When you'd grown out of them they used to be passed on to me—I can remember being very impatient for you to grow, sometimes, when you had a dress I really coveted.' Polly was laughing but Miranda looked uncertainly at her—had Polly ever resented that? 'Now I can buy my own but they never have that glamour, no matter how much they cost,' Polly added, then took the compress away and studied the bump closely. 'How does it feel?'

'Better,' Miranda lied, giving her a grateful look. 'My hair's a mess,' she said, staring at herself in the bathroom mirror.

'Borrow my comb,' Polly offered, perching on the bath to watch her cousin carefully tidying her dark brown hair. Miranda had a smooth, matt complexion and rather delicate features; a small straight nose, wide-set eyes, high cheekbones and a pink bow of a mouth.

'Do you like Sean?' Miranda asked suddenly, turning to give her cousin back the comb.

Polly looked disconcerted, her eyes widening. 'I hardly know him. He's a very attractive guy, that's all I've noticed.' She grinned, her auburn hair a riot of curls falling to her shoulders. Polly had a vibrant energy in her colouring as well as in her temperament. 'Lucky old you,' she added. 'Shall I hang around in case you grow out of him, too?'

It was a joke and Miranda laughed but her eyes were desolate as she turned away. Was it just her mood or was she reading far more between the lines of what was said to her than she ever had before? Had she been blind until now? Or was it simply that Diana's malice had worked its way under her skin and made her see the whole world differently?

Downstairs they stood in the doorway of the drawing-room listening to the hum of voices. Miranda's father stood on the other side of the room talking to Diana. Miranda stared at them, tense and alert, trying to read what was really going on under their surface smiles.

Ferdinand Boston was a powerfully built man in his late fifties; with a massive, leonine head of crisp grey hair which had once been the same dark brown as Miranda's. He had her blue eyes, too, and there any resemblance ended because she had inherited her bone structure and build from her delicate mother. Ferdy had obstinacy and tenacity in every line of his strongly featured face, the way he carried his head spoke of purpose and drive, it was set on his broad neck like a visible challenge, his jaw thrust out, his mouth firm and wide with a full lower lip.

He looked oddly out of place in the elegant drawing-room, although he had personally picked out everything it contained; choosing the restrained cream and gold of the walls and curtains, the deep-piled carpet and all the furniture, the brocade-covered suite, the mahogany table on which stood a cream-and-gold ormolu clock, the silk-shaded cream stone lamps.

Ferdy's strength and brooding physical presence did not fit the silken elegance around him, but Miranda knew how proud of this room he was—every time he looked at it his eyes glowed with the satisfaction of remembering that it was light years away from the London slums where he had grown up. They smiled like that when they looked at her, too, although she had often wondered if he would rather have had a son to run his hand-built empire.

With a prickle of alarm she suddenly remembered something he had said to her when she and Sean told him that they wanted to get married. Her father hadn't been surprised, she recalled. He had looked as if he knew what they were going to say before they said a word. He had beamed approvingly, standing on the hearth of this room, looming over them like a contented bear, his broad shoulders relaxed.

'Now I've got a son as well as a daughter,' he had said and Miranda had been so touched that she had flung her arms round him and kissed him, and Ferdy had said with a chuckle, 'I know you're going to be very happy with Sean, darling. You'd better be or I'll want to know the reason why! After all, I hand-picked him for you and I wouldn't want less than the best for my little girl.'

At the time she had laughed and leaned her head against Sean's arm, feeling cloudily self-conscious, aware of the two men eyeing each other over her head but not suspicious of any hidden meanings in what they said to each other. Why should she have any doubts? Ferdy liked to believe that everything that happened in his private world came about because he chose to make it happen. He had hand-picked her school, her clothes, her job in the company; deciding that she wasn't temperamentally suited to the hassle of business he had put her into the design department where she would be under no pressure, and he had been right. Miranda hadn't been attracted by the daily friction of the more go-ahead parts of the company; she enjoyed working in the spacious, sunlit offices of the design department. She was quite good at her work, and during her three years there she had been promoted twice—each time because she deserved the promotion, not because she was the daughter of the managing director. Miranda had always been good at art at school, and she had found commercial design for packaging and advertising a fascinating area of work. Her father might congratulate himself on picking the right job for her, but she knew she had been successful without his help and could easily get another job with a firm who wouldn't treat her as a special case.

'Who's the blonde?' Polly asked and Miranda started, having forgotten that her cousin was next to her. Following Polly's gaze she saw that the blonde she meant was Diana.

'My father's secretary, Diana Cobbold.'

'What's she like?'

Miranda hesitated. 'I hardly know her,' she evaded.

'Very flashy,' Polly murmured thoughtfully. 'All glam and glitter like a Woolworth's bracelet—when you scratch the gilt there's tin underneath.'

Miranda laughed and gave her cousin a grateful

smile. 'Yes, I know exactly what you mean.'

'Does she always flirt with Uncle Ferdy like that?' Polly asked with the directness Miranda envied but couldn't imitate. 'I may be wrong, but I'd say she's got her eye on him. I know he's on the wrong side of fifty, but she's the type to fancy herself as a rich man's pet and that wouldn't bother someone like her.'

Miranda pretended to laugh. 'I'll warn Daddy.'

One of her aunts came up to hug her, slightly tipsy after an evening of champagne and caviar. 'You're going to be a beautiful bride, Miranda, just like your mother—she was always the prettiest of us as well as the delicate one. I wish she could be here to see how lovely you are.'

'Thank you, Aunt Patsy,' Miranda said, kissing her cheek. 'I hope you're having a lovely time.' She was fond of all her mother's sisters.

'Oh, Ferdy always does these things so well. Your father is a marvellous man, Miranda.' Patsy Wood was a small, plump, comfortable woman with grey hair.

'I know he is,' Miranda said, a lump in her throat.

'The amazing thing is that he hasn't managed to spoil you. I've never known such a doting father. My George can hardly remember who our boys are. The other day one of them walked past and George said: "Who's that?"'

Polly giggled. 'I bet that was Johnny and you can't really blame Uncle George—Johnny *has* had his hair dyed pink since he went punk and started going around in those old dungarees.'

Patsy Wood gave a hoarse chuckle of amusement. 'Oh, he'll grow out of that. I must say, the pink hair made me jump, but you get used to it.'

'Not Uncle George, obviously,' Polly teased and their aunt laughed again.

'George is very conservative; he's forgotten he was ever young. That's something else I admire about your father, Miranda, he's stayed very young. He's enjoyed this evening so much—well, look at him now, having a great time with that crowd of young people. You're as young as you feel, that's what I always say, and my George feels about a hundred most of the time.'

Miranda turned away, ostensibly to take a glass of champagne from a tray being carried past by one of the waitresses her father had hired for the evening. Her hand shook and drops of wine fell on her cream silk dress as she lifted the glass to her mouth. Her father did look as if he was having a wonderful time, he had an arm around Diana as he roared with laughter at something she had just said, and his face was flushed with wine and excitement.

At that moment she caught her father's eye and he detached himself from Diana and the others around them to come over to her. 'Hallo, kitten—having a lovely party?' he asked, kissing her nose and then stared at her forehead, pushing aside the heavy lock of dark brown hair with which she had disguised the bump. 'What's that? How did you get that bruise?' At once his face was anxious, his blue eyes alert.

'I banged my head on a table,' she stammered and Polly came to her rescue.

'Too much champagne, I'm afraid,' she teased and Miranda pretended to laugh.

'Don't give me away, you rat!'

Ferdy Boston brushed the hair down again gently. 'Does it hurt? Why aren't you more careful? At least you'll be able to hide it with your hair—I don't want Sean complaining that I've sold him damaged goods.'

Everyone laughed—except Miranda, who stared at the floor with a pale face, struggling with a rush of angry anxiety. Only a few hours ago she would have been laughing with the others, she would have taken her father's remark for a joke with no hidden meaning.

'You're very quiet, got a headache?' her father asked and with relief she nodded.

'I think I ought to go to bed,' she said and everyone laughed again.

'Wedding day nerves starting early,' Aunt Patsy said.

'If I was marrying Sean Hinton, I'd have wedding day nerves,' said Polly. 'I don't mind admitting, I'm green with envy, Miranda. He's gorgeous.'

'Of course he is, I picked him,' Ferdy said complacently and Miranda turned away.

'I'd better go and say good night to everyone,' she muttered and began to make the rounds of all her friends and relatives, kissing and being kissed, and smiling fixedly at every joke. Nobody seemed to notice except one man whose face was vaguely familiar although she couldn't quite remember having met him before.

'You look very hassled, don't let it get to you,' he said as she shyly nodded around the group of which he was a part, and Miranda froze as she recognised his voice. It was the man who had been in the library with Diana.

'I don't think we've met, have we?' she asked, her voice brittle.

He held out his hand, smiling with a lazy charm that was only skin deep; his hazel eyes were too much like Diana's. 'I'm Paul Cobbold— my cousin is your father's secretary. I'm one of your firm's sales reps.' He smiled again. 'Keep it in the family is a good motto, as your father was saying earlier.'

'We're a family firm,' Miranda said, 'Good night, thank you for coming.' She walked away very carefully, fighting to keep the calmness in her face. Inside, her mind was filled with questions—how much of what Diana had said was the truth? How much was a lie twisted to sound like the truth?

Had her father struck a bargain with Sean? Was her marriage an arranged one, secretly planned behind her back?

She met Ferdy Boston at the door and said quietly: 'I'm going up to bed now, Daddy, but I'd like to talk to you for five minutes, please.'

He smiled indulgently. 'Last minute qualms? They'll pass.'

'Just five minutes, Daddy,' she said with something of his own insistence and he nodded, putting an arm around her to lead her up the stairs.

'I'm only just beginning to realise that tonight is the last night when you'll be here when I come home,' he said on a sigh. 'I'm going to be very lonely, I hope I'll still see quite a bit of you, Miranda. I wouldn't want to lose you to Sean altogether.'

'You won't,' she promised, leading him into her bedroom. She sat down on the bed, her hands in her lap, watching him. 'Daddy, why didn't you ever marry again?' she asked suddenly and saw his surprised face. He hadn't been expecting that.

'I suppose I never met anyone I wanted to marry,' he said, sitting down next to her. 'Look, darling, don't worry about what I said just now— I'm too busy to be lonely very often and I'll always be able to drop in on you and Sean from time to time when I'm feeling low, won't I? Don't fret your head over me.' He took her hands and patted them, smiling. 'I'm tougher than I look!'

She smiled back nervously. 'Tonight someone said something about Mummy making you promise not to marry, that's all.' She watched his eyes narrow.

'My God, how women talk! Who was it? Your Aunt Patsy? She should have known better.'

'Was it true, though?' she pressed.

He shrugged, getting up. 'Your mother had some sort of fixation about it. I promised her not to re-marry while you were young, that's all there was to it. It really wasn't important, don't go getting any idea that I sacrificed my happiness for you: I never met anyone I wanted to marry,

I've been too busy and I'm not really the domesticated sort. I've been very happy as I am, thank you.' He walked towards the door. 'Happy now, you goose?'

'Daddy, after the wedding, don't I inherit those shares?' she asked and he looked round, his expression whimsical.

'Don't you ever listen? The lawyers explained all that to you when you and Sean got engaged— the shares will be in trust for your children and Sean will manage the trust fund. I don't know why we bothered to explain it all to you, it obviously went in one ear and out the other.'

'Did you want me to marry Sean, Daddy?' she asked in a clear, quiet voice, watching him.

'You know I did. You couldn't have chosen anyone I approved of more, my pet. I used to have nightmares when I thought of you marrying some guy who might ruin the company, but I know I can safely leave everything in Sean's hands. He's a formidable guy.'

Miranda lowered her lashes and watched him through them. 'So you picked him out for me?' she asked casually, pretending to laugh.

Her father laughed, too, not hearing the note in her voice which betrayed something other than amusement.

'Just call me Cupid.' He opened the door and blew her a kiss. 'Now, get to bed and sleep well. Tomorrow is the biggest day in your life, remember.'

When the door had closed and he was gone, she sat staring at the empty air, her face tense, trying to think clearly. If her father had really arranged her marriage, Sean couldn't be in love with her. She shifted on the bed, trembling. She didn't believe that, Sean did love her—how could he have been pretending all these months? They had been seeing each other for six months now. They had got engaged three months ago, she had seen Sean two or three times a week throughout those months and she simply didn't believe he could have been acting.

Couldn't he? asked that cold voice inside her head. What makes you so sure?

She deliberately summoned up pictures of Sean kissing her, holding her hand in a theatre, chasing her while she laughed as they ran barefoot on a beach. She had been lighthearted with happiness, she had believed Sean felt the same.

There's only one thing to do, she thought. I'll ask him outright and then I'll be quite sure.

And when will you do that? the voice enquired drily, and her eyes darkened in realisation. There was no time to discuss this with Sean. She was getting married at eleven o'clock tomorrow. She looked at her watch. It was nearly one in the morning—just ten hours from now she would be arriving at the church. She wouldn't see Sean until they met at the altar and once they were actually married it would be too late to start asking him any of these questions.

What would happen if she asked Sean to postpone the wedding? Panic ran through her at the very idea of the reaction she would get from

Sean, from her father. They would brush aside her doubts, laugh her out of what they would see as an attack of last-minute nerves. After all, what reason did she really have for suddenly being uncertain? An overheard conversation full of spiteful remarks and innuendo—she had no real proof that Diana had been telling the truth.

Quickly her mind reminded her that Diana had been right about something—Ferdy had promised her mother not to marry again until Miranda was grown up, and he had obviously badly wanted Miranda to marry Sean.

She couldn't sit here all night brooding and worrying while the moment of her wedding came closer and closer. Time was running out and she had to make a decision.

She could hear the sound of cars driving away, raised voices outside the house. The party was breaking up, people were leaving in droves.

She had to get away, give herself more time to think where she would be safe from the sort of pressure her father and Sean would bring to bear once they knew what was in her mind. She looked at her elegant cream silk dress, her face confused. She should never have agreed to that big party. She stripped and hunted for a pair of jeans and a thick sweater, while she tried to work out where to go. She had to talk to someone— someone neutral, outside the family, who would be ready to listen without trying to railroad her into a decision. But who?

While she packed a small suitcase she ran through the names of her friends, but most of them were Sean's friends too, she couldn't be certain that they would be on her side. Clare? she thought, her face brightening. Of course—Clare. Miranda had only kept in close touch with one of her old schoolfriends, Clare Holm. Clare had been invited to the wedding and she lived in a small flat a few miles away. Clare was unconventional, broad-minded, clear-headed. Miranda knew she would be able to talk to her frankly and get some sound advice which was unbiased.

The house was very quiet when she softly opened her door. She had written a brief note to her father saying that she was sorry but she couldn't go through with the marriage; she hadn't been able to say any more.

As she stole down the stairs the house creaked and whispered and her nerves prickled uneasily, she kept looking over her shoulder, expecting to see her father on the landing, hear him coming after her. She opened the front door with great care and threw a last look back, hesitating. Was she making a bad mistake? Should she go back, marry Sean and then . . .

She closed her eyes, shuddering. How could she do that? She would never be happy while these doubts were seething in her mind. However much trouble she caused by doing it this way at least she would not have committed the error of marrying a man who didn't really love her and only wanted control of her father's company. If Sean did love her, surely he would understand, when everything had cooled down? He must see that she had had no choice.

She closed the door softly and walked hurriedly down the street in the quiet of a March morning. On the corner she caught a taxi and gave him Clare's address. It was only as they drove off that she realised how little money she had with her. She would just have enough to pay the taxi. She sank back into the seat, her head beating with anxiety and pain, hoping she had done the right thing.

CHAPTER TWO

MIRANDA had to ring the doorbell several times before she saw a light come on and heard footsteps coming down the corridor. Clare opened the door a moment later and stared in amazement. 'Miranda?' she said in an incredulous voice, the drowsiness going out of her face. She was wearing a casually tied dressing-gown and her feet were bare, Miranda had obviously got her out of bed.

'I'm sorry to wake you up but I've got to talk to someone,' Miranda said keeping her voice low so as not to disturb the tenants of the other flats.

Clare gave her a searching look, then stepped back. 'Come in.' She waved Miranda into the small kitchen, switching on the light. 'Come in here—I'll make us some coffee. Park yourself.' She switched on an electric kettle and spooned instant coffee granules into two mugs, watching Miranda observantly. 'I suppose you haven't got amnesia and forgotten that you're getting married tomorrow?' she asked drily, then looked at the kitchen clock, pulling a face. 'Or, rather, today! It's gone two in the morning.'

'Something's happened,' Miranda said and Clare smiled.

'I did rather suspect it.' She was a tall, willowy girl with rough brown hair and steadfast brown eyes; you could read Clare's nature in those calm, unflappable eyes.

'I didn't know who else to go to,' stammered Miranda. 'I had to talk to someone, I don't know what to do.'

Clare poured the boiling water into the two mugs, stirred them and handed one to Miranda. She sat down at the table opposite her, hands clasped around the mug of steaming coffee, sipped carefully and sighed.

'That's better—I feel more human now.' She looked at Miranda encouragingly. 'So what's the problem and how can I help?'

Miranda took a deep breath, her face very pale. 'It started at the party tonight. I had to get away from them all. My family *en masse* can be exhausting. I went into the library, it was the only room that wasn't overrun with people.'

Clare listened intently, her eyes fixed on Miranda's face, occasionally drinking some coffee, and Miranda told her what she had overheard and what she had found out later. Her voice was low and ragged and she paused from time to time as she tried to make a coherent story out of what seemed even to her to be a confused series of conversations.

When she finally trailed off into silence, Clare studied her wryly. 'I'm not very interested in what this secretary said or what any of your aunts told you or even what your father may have said. Only one question really matters—do you love Sean?'

Miranda looked at her, the dark pupils of her

eyes dilated. 'Yes,' she said with unsteady lips. 'I love him, but . . .' she broke off, swallowing.

'But does he really love you?' Clare shrewdly finished for her, brows lifted.

Miranda nodded and reached blindly for the mug of coffee. It had cooled sufficiently for her to be able to drink it. Clare had made it strong; it tasted bitter to her but she drank it all the same.

'It seems to me that you must have had doubts before tonight,' Clare said gently. 'You wouldn't have thought twice about overhearing a spiteful woman's remarks if they hadn't touched on a nerve.'

Miranda looked at her, frowning, but didn't argue because she knew that that must be obvious. She hadn't allowed herself to think too deeply about her doubts, but at the back of her mind she had often wondered if Sean really cared for her with the same fierce passion she felt for him. She didn't even know what it was that had put those doubts into her head in the beginning. It had been intangible, a vague feeling that Sean was marrying her because she made a suitable wife, rather than because he couldn't live without her.

'I'm not really the person you should be talking to, am I?' Cláre asked her with a smile. 'You've got to talk to Sean himself.'

'But would he tell me the truth? If Diana wasn't lying—if my father and Sean did more or less arrange my marriage without letting me guess—then Sean won't admit it, will he?'

Clare gave her a shrewd look. 'You don't really

know him all that well, do you? The only couple of times I met him he seemed almost too direct, even curt. I hadn't written him down as the type to lie.'

Mirada looked confused. 'No, that's true, he isn't.' She paused, biting her lip. 'But how can I go ahead with the marriage when I feel so muddled about it all?'

'Marriage is a big step, it isn't surprising if you feel bemused and suddenly not so sure that you want to go through with it. It's never easy to make big decisions, but if you've made one and something happens to put doubts into your mind, that can throw you into a panic.'

Miranda put a hand to her head. 'I've got a terrible headache,' she muttered. 'You're so sensible, Clare, I wish I was as level-headed as you are.'

Clare laughed slightly ruefully. 'You make me sound very dull.'

'Sorry, I didn't mean to,' Miranda said, smiling, although the pain in her head was making it difficult for her to see properly. 'I think I've got migraine,' she said with a wince.

Clare got up. 'I've got some pills for that— they'll help you get to sleep, too. I'll set the alarm clock for eight o'clock and that will give you time to make a final decision about whether or not you want to go through with your wedding tomorrow.'

She ran the cold tap and filled a glass, found a small pink box of pills and shook two into Miranda's hand. 'Take those and then get off to bed. My spare room is small but there are clean sheets on the bed. My mother said she might come for the weekend tomorrow and I made the bed up for her.'

'I'm very grateful to you for listening,' Miranda said as she lifted a pill to her mouth. She took both pills, drank a little more water, and handed the glass back to Clare. 'Thank you.'

Clare walked back down the corridor with her. 'Have you got a nightie in your case?'

Miranda nodded. 'I just threw a few things into it and crept out. I didn't even remember to bring any money, I only just had enough to pay the taxi driver. He looked pretty grim when he saw the size of the tip which was all I had left.'

Clare laughed. 'He'll get over it. I can lend you anything you need.'

'You are good,' Miranda said, hugging her.

'You'd do the same for me!'

'Any day!' Miranda promised.

'Although I doubt if I'll ever have such a bizarre problem,' Clare said. 'My father takes no interest in my love life—his only obsession is his budgerigars.' She looked dubiously around the small but tidy room. 'It isn't what you're used to, I'm afraid.'

'It's just what I need right now,' Miranda said on a sigh. 'A quiet place where I can think without feeling pressured. I couldn't do my thinking at home; I kept hearing the clocks ticking.'

'You're not even to try to think!' Clare ordered. 'Sleep—that's what you need. You can do all your worrying tomorrow.'

She went out and Miranda slowly undressed, feeling lethargic and stupid, slipped into the narrow bed and put out the light. She had no sooner put her head on the pillow than her heavy lids dropped over her eyes. A few minutes later she was asleep

She woke up suddenly, hearing loud voices, and struggled up on to her elbow to look at the clock on the bedside table. It was half-past eight, the room was filling slowly with grey daylight, but she felt as if she had only been asleep for half an hour. For a second she was totally disorientated, she looked around the unfamiliar little room, blinking, stifling a yawn, and then memory rushed back and she knew where she was and what had happened to bring her here.

Half-past eight? she suddenly thought. My God, Clare promised to wake me up at eight, she must have overslept. She swung herself out of the bed hurriedly. The voices had risen, Miranda vaguely noticed, only to come awake with a jab of alarm as it dawned on her that one of the voices was only too familiar to her.

'Sean,' she whispered, stiffening. It couldn't be! What was he doing here? Surely Clare hadn't got in touch with him? Clare wouldn't do that to her.

She crept to the door, listening. Sean's voice had a harsh, grating quality she had never heard in it before, her nerves quivered as she recognised the rage in that tone.

'Will you take the chain off this door or do I have to kick it down?'

'I would not advise that,' Clare said calmly. 'You wouldn't want to spend your wedding day in police custody, would you?'

There was a silence then the sound of Sean's voice. 'She is here, though, isn't she? Don't you think I have a right to talk to her?'

'What I think doesn't matter,' Clare said. 'It's what Miranda thinks that counts.'

'Miranda!' Sean shouted.

'For heaven's sake, keep your voice down,' Clare said impatiently. 'You'll wake the whole building up. It's only half-past eight in the morning, remember!'

Sean ignored her. 'Miranda! I'm not leaving until I've talked to you so come out here and tell your watchdog to take the chain off her door.'

Miranda's heart was thudding violently. She felt perspiration trickling down her back, between her breasts. Her face was icy white, though, she felt as if she might faint. Her hesitation was only momentary. She couldn't let Sean kick up a scene on Clare's doorstep. She would have liked time to nerve herself up to facing him, but time had just run out. She pulled open the door.

Clare glanced back over her shoulder. 'You don't have to see him if you don't want to, Miranda,' she said. 'I can ring the police and have him removed, if that's what you want.'

'Why don't you mind your own business?' Sean snarled.

Clare gave him a cool look. 'I've known Miranda since she was seven. She came here for refuge, that makes it my business. What good will it do to bully her when she's obviously off balance? If you shout at her the way you've been shouting at me you'll just make matters worse.'

Miranda began to walk slowly down the corridor. Sean watched her through the slit of door, his dark eyes glittering.

'Take this chain off,' he demanded and Clare looked round at Miranda, her brows lifting in question.

'Shall I?'

'He's right, I'd better talk to him,' Miranda said jerkily.

Clare shrugged and unhooked the chain. Sean was through the door a second later and Miranda hurried into the small sitting-room with him hard on her heels. Clare stood in the doorway. 'If you need a referee I'll be within earshot,' she promised.

'We won't,' Sean said curtly.

'I wasn't talking to you.'

Miranda gave her friend a wry little smile. 'I'll be okay, thanks, Clare.'

Clare closed the door and Miranda stood, rooted to the spot, her breath coming in a shallow, frightened way while she waited for Sean to say something. She had no idea what to say to him; her wits had deserted her. It was only at that minute that she realised that all she had on was a thin cotton nightdress and hot colour flowed into her face. Hearing Sean's voice had driven everything else out of her head. She wished she had stopped to put on a dressing gown.

He was staring at her, his lean body pulsating with the rage she had heard earlier when he was shouting at Clare. Now that they were alone, he seemed as uncertain where to start as Miranda herself. She looked at him through her lashes and felt her heart miss a beat. Whenever she saw Sean she felt her body responding helplessly to the physical magnetism of his male sexuality. She had never met any other man who made her so aware of his masculinity. Sean wasn't good-looking; his face was too strongly featured, it suggested force more than good looks. His nose had been broken during a rugger game when he was a boy and it had set slightly crooked. His dark eyes were the only beauty in that face, they had a deep lustre that riveted the eye, if you looked into them you were lured into forgetting the hard power of the jawline, the firm, cool mouth. His black hair was ruffled now, as though he had just got out of bed, but normally he wore it brushed down smoothly and tapering into his nape. Although he was a tall man he moved with an assurance that came close to grace and he kept very fit, playing squash and tennis and in the autumn turning out for an amateur rugby club.

'Why?' he suddenly broke out and her throat beat with panic. 'Why did you do it? There hadn't been a sign of any doubts, you hadn't given so much as a hint that you weren't certain . . . why, in God's name?'

She felt her legs becoming weak and sat down to give herself time to gather her thoughts. 'How did you find me?' she asked huskily.

Sean laughed shortly. 'Your father couldn't sleep and went down to get himself some warm milk—he saw your light on and wondered if you were awake too.'

Miranda caught her breath. How stupid—she must have forgotten to switch off the light in her room before she left.

'Was he . . .?'

'Worried? What do you think? When he had read your note he rang me, in quite a state. I went round to your house and we started looking for you. We rang all the obvious places first— your aunts, your cousins.' He gave her a hard, cold stare. 'You certainly caused quite a sensation; half your family were up worrying about you last night.'

'I'm sorry,' she stammered and was given a sarcastic stare.

'Are you? Pity you didn't think of the consequences before you walked out, isn't it? We might never have found you if I hadn't suddenly thought of Clare Holm and remembered that she was the only one of your schoolfriends who kept in touch with you. I rang her an hour ago—she didn't admit you were here, but she didn't seem surprised by my call. All the others had been— they had all been stunned. She was too calm, I suspected she was being evasive, so I drove round here.'

'I had to have time to think,' Miranda said in a low voice and he leaned down to hear her, his powerful body looming over her and making her nervous.

'Think? About what, for heaven's sake?'

'Don't shout at me,' she said, bristling.

She heard the deep breath he took, felt his body vibrating with anger. 'You walk out on me on our wedding day and then tell me not to shout at you?'

She flinched, sinking deeper into the corner of the couch, and Sean stared at her, his hands clenched at his side, his nostrils flaring in an effort to keep his temper. He swung away from her suddenly.

'I'd better ring your father and tell him I've found you or he'll have the police out looking for you. He thinks you've had some sort of brainstorm and may be wandering about in a dazed state. He's out of his mind with worry, although I don't suppose that will bother you.'

'Of course it does,' she burst out, shaking.

Sean gave her a sardonic look, hostility in the barb of his smile. 'Really?' he disputed and opened the door. Clare was hovering in the corridor. 'Eavesdropping?' Sean enquired nastily but didn't wait for her to deny it. 'Where's your 'phone? I have to ring her father and put his mind at rest.'

'In my bedroom,' Clare said, pointing, and Sean strode off down the corridor. Clare came into the sitting-room, looking quickly at Miranda. 'Are you okay?'

Miranda nodded without saying anything.

'At least he hasn't strangled you,' Clare said with a dry humour which Miranda did not find amusing. 'I've made some coffee—want some?'

'Please!' Miranda's mouth was so dry, she could hardly swallow.

Clare came back a moment later with a cup of coffee and as Miranda took it they heard Sean's rapid stride returning. Clare turned. 'Would you like some coffee?' she asked and Sean shook his head.

'I've been drinking the stuff all night, I couldn't look at another cup.'

Clare shrugged and removed herself, closing the door behind her. Miranda drank some coffee, her eyes lowered.

'Now, perhaps you'll tell me why you ran away and what that terse note meant?' Sean demanded, standing in front of her, his hands plunged into his pockets. Through her lowered lashes she noted the casual clothes he wore; black cord pants and a matching cord jacket elasticated at the waist. As she watched he unzipped the jacket and left it open; under it he wore a white silk shirt, open at the neck.

'I told you, I suddenly couldn't ... I didn't know if I ...' Her voice broke down and he watched her, frowning, then leaned down and took the cup away, putting it on a table.

'Are you trying to say that you don't want to marry me, after all?' he asked harshly. 'That you've changed your mind? You don't love me?'

She tried to think clearly but his presence was too confusing, how could she think when all she was conscious of was Sean's powerful, male body and the way it made her feel?

Sean shifted, his breathing impatient, and she

started again: 'How do I know you want to marry me and not just my father's daughter?' she whispered. 'You want to control the company, don't you, Sean? Is that why you're marrying me?'

He stiffened and she involuntarily looked up to see what effect her questions had had—she wished she had kept her eyes down a second later as she met the dangerous flash of those gleaming dark eyes. They probed her face like black steel darts seeking out her vulnerable places and she winced away, her lashes fluttering against her hot cheeks.

'So,' he said slowly on a long breath. 'That's it. You think I'm marrying you for your money?'

'My father's money,' she said bitterly because her father had been part of this conspiracy too.

'It comes to the same thing, doesn't it? Ferdy wouldn't leave any of it to anyone else—you know he loves the ground you walk on!' Then Sean's anger flamed up again and he asked bitingly: 'How could you do this to him? We'll leave me out of it as you seem so uncertain how you feel about me—but your father loves you more than life itself, how could you do this to him? Don't you know he's been out of his mind with worry ever since he found you had gone? All sorts of crazy ideas have been going round in his head. He said you were in a strange mood last night, talking oddly, asking weird questions, but he put it down to wedding nerves. When he found you'd gone, though, he remembered that you'd bumped your head that night and he wondered if you had got concussion. He imagined you wandering around, getting run over by some car, being mugged ... God knows what.'

'I'm sorry if he has been worried, I wasn't thinking clearly.'

'Obviously not,' he said with force.

'I didn't know what to do! I had to think, but the time was so short, and if I'd stayed I knew that my father wouldn't have listened to me, he would have made me go through with the wedding and I couldn't face it.'

'You left it a bit late to realise that you couldn't stand the idea of being married to me, didn't you?' he asked in a voice which was barely under control. Miranda couldn't look at him, he scared her too much, but she felt the brooding fixity of his anger without needing to see his face.

'It happened too fast,' she began and suddenly Sean's control snapped. He bent and gripped her arms, pulled her up from the couch while her agitated eyes lifted in shock to his face.

'What are you doing?' she stammered, her throat closing in alarm.

'Let's try a little experiment,' he said and Miranda shivered in protest, realising what he meant to do as his mouth lowered towards her own.

'No!' she broke out, but had no chance to say any more. His mouth closed over hers while it was parted and she was helpless to avoid that deep, sensual invasion. A shudder of heated response ran through her, she was dizzy with intense feeling, her hands clutching his shoulders and her head thrown back under the demanding force of the kiss. Sean slid a hand down her spine, pressing her closer, and her body obeyed without her volition, melting against him until there was no space between their bodies.

When he finally lifted his head she was shaking violently, hanging on to him to stay upright, her eyes closed and her head spinning. Sean always had that devastating effect on her senses; she ached with desire, waiting for him to kiss her again, her mouth lifted, parted and trembling.

'Well, well,' he said oddly and her eyes snapped open, the dissolving sweetness flowing out of her body as her mind began to operate again. Her face burnt as she looked at him. His mouth was crooked with mockery and his dark eyes surveyed her as though she puzzled him.

'Would you call that a very convincing display of indifference?' he drawled and she pushed him away.

'That has nothing to do with it,' she muttered in confusion.

His brows rose. 'I'd have said it had everything to do with it.'

'There's more to marriage than sexual attraction.' She defied him, her chin lifted. 'I can't trust you.'

His eyes hardened and narrowed, his mouth compressing. 'Can't trust me?' he repeated, a slow stain of red seeping into his face. A clock chimed softly in the silence that followed while their eyes argued, and Sean looked away, frowning, to study his watch. 'It's half-past nine,' he said through tight lips, then he caught hold of her arm and hustled her towards the door.

'What are you doing?' Miranda asked, torn between anger and anxiety.

'You're getting dressed and we're going back to your home.' Sean pushed her down the corridor and Clare appeared in the kitchen doorway, staring at them. Sean thrust Miranda through the open door of the little bedroom and came in after her.

'Will you get dressed or do I have to dress you?'

She backed. 'I'm not going, I can't, you can't make me.'

'Watch me,' he challenged softly.

'Sean, I'm serious—I can't marry you.'

His mouth hardened, the faint smile going. He looked around the room, found the little heap of her clothes and moved towards them, purpose in his stride. Miranda felt her pulses beating hard.

'Okay, I'll get dressed,' she said hurriedly, unable to face the thought of Sean forcibly dressing her. 'But not until you've gone out of here. I'm not putting on my clothes with you watching me.'

'Why not?' he asked in dry mockery. 'After today you're going to have to get used to it.'

'I won't marry you!' she insisted.

He walked to the door. 'I'll give you five minutes and then I'm coming back in here and if you aren't dressed I'll have that nightdress off and put some clothes on you myself. One way or another, Miranda, you're coming back to face your father. Perhaps you'll be able to explain to him what the hell is going on inside your head. So far you haven't given me a clue.'

The door slammed and she shakily went over to bolt it but there was no bolt, nor was there a key. Her shoulders slumping, she went back to pick up her clothes and changed as quickly as she could, her fingers trembling as she pulled the sweater over her head and smoothed it down. She could hear Sean talking to Clare who sounded angry; no doubt Clare had asked him what was happening and why he was pushing Miranda around as if she were a child. Miranda resented the overbearing way he had hustled her down the corridor and bullied her into getting dressed, but she was reserving her energy for the conflict to come when she faced both Sean and her father and tried to explain why she had changed her mind about getting married.

The one thing she could not do was tell them that she had overheard Diana's conversation—if she told them that they would simply deny everything and try to railroad her into going through with the wedding. They had to believe that this was her own decision, that she was serious, and knew what she was doing. If they imagined that she was merely reacting to malicious gossip, they wouldn't listen. They wouldn't realise—as she had realised long before Clare mentioned it to her—that Diana's bitchy remarks had made some sort of bitter sense to her. At the back of her mind, she had felt uneasy about Sean's real feelings towards her for months. There was so much about him that raised questions in her mind—a cool, astute determination to succeed, an unhidden ambition, a trace of ruthless will. He had rarely shown them to her, it was true; but over the past months she had glimpsed them without ever letting herself think too deeply about what they implied.

She had been too blindly in love with him; if she had been hoodwinked, she had co-operated with him to make it possible. She hadn't wanted to know what sort of man he really was; her feverish sensual involvement with him had driven her on into committing herself without ever questioning Sean's committment. She had gone on like someone walking a high wire over a precipice, not daring to look down, keeping her eyes fixed ahead. She had known, deep down, that there was empty air below her, though, hadn't she? She had suspected it, at least, but she had rushed on without stopping to think because she had wanted him so desperately.

Her eyes burst with humiliation and pain as she remembered the way she had kissed him back a moment or two ago. She had given in to her own desire, reather than to Sean's forceful kiss, but Sean had known exactly what he was doing to her. She winced at the memory of his mocking dark eyes, the satisfied gleam they held.

How was she going to convince him that, despite her helpless response, she still meant what she said?

The door opened and she started, running shaky hands over her dark hair. Sean threw an all-encompassing glance over her, his mouth wry.

'Ready?'

Clare was behind him, her face flushed after her argument with Sean. 'You don't have to go with him, you know,' she said. 'Don't let him push you into anything you're going to regret.'

'We haven't got time for any more discussions,' Sean told Miranda, and she felt the drag of his will power focused on her, those lustrous dark eyes brilliant with intent.

'Miranda, you don't have to do anything you don't want to do,' Clare insisted.

'She knows that,' said Sean, putting an arm around Miranda's slender shoulders and moving her towards the front door.

She detached herself and hugged Clare. 'Thanks for everything—I might as well go, you see. I have to talk to my father.'

'Don't let them browbeat you into a marriage you don't really want,' said Clare.

'She wants it,' Sean informed her curtly.

'Oh, yes? Is that why she ran away?' Clare was bristling like a hedgehog. 'Can't you see she needs more time?'

'She's not a child—she's a woman of twenty-two and she doesn't need advice from you.' Sean propelled Miranda through the door. 'See you at the church,' he said sarcastically over his shoulder and Clare glared after them, her hands on her hips.

Sean drove back to Miranda's home at a speed which made her grip the seat nervously, she could almost smell the burning tyres as he screeched around corners on three wheels.

'Slow down,' she said in agitation. 'Did you have to be so rude to Clare?'

'She annoyed me.'

'She's a very old friend of mine and you had no right to talk to her that way. She was only showing her concern for me.'

'She doesn't like men much, does she?' Sean said, his face impatient, taking another corner at high speed. The car seemed to lean over so far that Miranda caught her breath, expecting them to crash and turn over, but a moment later they were driving on quite safely although he didn't drop his speed. 'She's one of the aggressive breed of feminists who take every opportunity to attack any man they meet,' he added.

'What nonsense,' Miranda muttered. 'You don't know her—just because she doesn't like you . . .'

'She made that clear—is she behind all this? What has she been putting into your head? Telling you that I'm only marrying you for your money? Do you know what she said to me just now? She had the nerve to ask me if I'd made a bargain with your father before I asked you to marry me! Was it you—or the company—I wanted, she had the gall to ask. She was lucky I didn't lose my temper, or I'd have hit her.'

Miranda looked sideways at him, tense in her seat. Clare had been more direct than she had dared to be, she had asked him outright the very question Miranda wanted to ask.

'And what did you tell her?' she said in a dry voice and Sean shot her a hard stare; his features taut and hostile, the powerful structure of his face making her stomach clench in alarm.

'Don't provoke me, Miranda,' he said through those tightly compressed lips, his voice biting out each word. He turned into the drive of her home under the horse chestnut trees which were still almost bare, apart from the shiny, sticky buds sprouting here and there on the branches. Flushed, Miranda watched the broad façade of the red-brick house approaching. The green lawns were rimed with frost which was just beginning to melt in the warmth of the spring sunshine.

She stared at the house with a glaze of unshed tears over her eyes. Sean pulled up outside and rested an arm on the steering wheel while he turned to look at her. She lowered her eyes to hide the betraying trace of tears, but he took her chin between the fingers of one hand and gently wiped her eyes with a clean handkerchief.

'Try to remember that your father is almost sixty,' he said coolly. 'He wants grandchildren while he's still young enough to enjoy them, and he's worried about the chance that he might die and leave both you and the company without the sort of protection he wants for you.'

Huskily she whispered, 'Is that why the two of you made a bargain? You promised to take care of me and the company for him, did you?'

'I've promised him he need never worry about you again,' Sean said and she could almost see the care with which he picked the words. He was tacitly admitting that her accusation was true—he was marrying her for the company. Her heart lurched in pain.

Sean watched her for a second, then his eyes slid sideways to where the front door of the house had opened and his face altered. 'There's your father. Miranda, he has his heart set on this marriage. Remember that, before you make any drastic decisions. I think you would be happy with me. At the moment, you're in an emotional state, you're confused. Last minute panic isn't all that uncommon at weddings.' He smiled wryly down at her. 'A pity you didn't come out with all this weeks ago, we could have had more time to talk it out. Now, we only have an hour. You can't cancel all the arrangements now.' He mocked her, his eyes coaxing. 'Think of all the presents we'd have to send back, the invitations we'd have to cancel at such short notice. You can't leave me standing at the altar.'

Her eyes were bitter as she stared back at him. 'Can't I?' She got out of the car and her father hurried forward. He looked so pale and drawn that a rush of guilt swept over her.

'Miranda!' he said, putting his arms around her. It was only at that moment that she realised how worried he had been. He had always seemed such a strong man—ageless and unchanging, in spite of his silvery grey hair and the lines on his face. For the first time she realised just how old her father was—he seemed to her to have added years to his life during the night. He held her tightly, as though he had begun to think he would never see her again, and she shivered as she faced the fact that she was going to have to go through with her marriage to Sean. It was too late to back out now, Sean was right. If she did, it would hurt her father too much, and although she resented the private bargain he had struck with Sean she realised that he had been trying to protect her, make certain that she was safe and happy.

She could say to him: you had no right to arrange my life like that! But his intentions had been good and she loved her father too much to start a serious quarrel with him over an action which had sprung from his own love for her.

'How could you?' he muttered huskily.

'I'm sorry,' she said.

He held her away, looking down into her face. 'Are you all right?' His eyes were brilliant with anxiety and distress.

'Yes,' she said and Sean moved beside them, his attitude watchful.

'She's okay, Ferdy. The panic's over, but if she isn't going to be late at the church she ought to go straight upstairs and get dressed.' His voice was calm and level and Ferdy Boston looked at him helplessly.

'The wedding is still on, then?' He looked back at Miranda as he spoke but it was Sean who answered for her before she had time to open her mouth.

'It's going ahead as planned.'

Ferdy Boston gave a sigh and Miranda saw the relief in his face. She turned towards the house, her features rigidly controlled, only a fixed darkness in her blue eyes giving away any of the turmoil inside her. She was going to have to go through with this mockery of a wedding, there was no escape for her unless she was ready to break with her father, and she did not know how she was going to cope with being Sean's wife while she knew he did not love her.

Their panic might be over—but hers had just begun.

CHAPTER THREE

IT was not until she stood at the altar beside Sean, in a cold spring sunlight, that it really dawned on her what she was doing and what had happened to the excited dreams which had filled her waking and sleeping hours for weeks past. She heard her own voice repeating those hollow vows, felt Sean's fingers clasping her hand and wished she dared to break free and run out of the church, away from this travesty of all her hopes.

She hadn't had a moment to herself since she walked back into her home. Her aunts and several of her cousins had been there, waiting, on tenterhooks to know whether the wedding was on or off. They had taken one look at her face and then tactfully been silent. Aunt Ann had firmly bustled her upstairs while the two other aunts made sure that the bridesmaids were ready.

Polly had come into her bedroom half an hour later with a glass of brandy. 'Drink this,' she had said, pushing it into Miranda's hand, and Miranda, white-faced, had looked at it blankly.

'Go on, you don't want to faint in the church, do you?'

'It will make me sick.'

'No, it won't, just drink it and stop arguing.' Polly had given her a coaxing grin. 'It will help you through the day,' she said and Miranda had somehow dredged up a mimicry of a smile from somewhere.

'Oh, well, in that case . . .'

As she lifted the brandy glass to her lips, Polly stood behind her, watching their joint reflections in the long mirror. The shimmer of Miranda's ivory satin dress had more colour than her face, but as the brandy hit the back of her throat she shuddered, turning pink. A moment later the heat of the spirit was circulating in her blood and she began to feel faintly dizzy. She hadn't eaten anything that morning, she realised; the only thing she had drunk was the cup of coffee which Clare had given her.

'I don't think I should have drunk brandy on an empty stomach,' she said ruefully, and Polly had exclaimed with impatience.

'You mean you haven't had any breakfast? Really, Miranda, you're an idiot, why didn't you say so?'

'I'll get her something,' Aunt Ann had said, moving quickly to the door. 'Miranda, don't for heaven's sake sit down in that dress or it will crease before you get to the church.'

Miranda had averted her eyes from the image of herself she saw in the mirror and looked instead at her cousin. 'You look marvellous, Polly—you were right, that colour was perfect for you.'

Polly was her chief bridesmaid and had helped her to choose the colour and style of the dress all the bridesmaids were to wear. Polly had frankly demanded a delicate lemon shade; it would suit the others well enough and would help to mute the vibrant colouring of Polly's auburn hair. It had been Polly, too, who had picked out the coronet of seed pearls set in delicate filigree silver mesh which the bridesmaids were to wear on their heads.

'The car's here and Uncle Ferdy is pacing the hall, waiting for the signal to be off,' Polly had said cheerfully, but she had been watching Miranda all the time and her eyes had been far more sober than her light tone.

Miranda had not looked at the clock but she had heard it softly ticking away the minutes until she left this house and began the misery of being Sean's wife, knowing that he did not love her.

'You look lovely, you know,' Polly had said gently. 'That dress is so romantic.'

Miranda's lips twisted in an involuntary, bitter smile. That was why she had chosen it—because the design was so romantic. A heart-shaped neckline, long full sleeves fastened at the wrist with pearl drops, a tight-fitting waist and rustling, sweeping skirts under which she wore several layers of stiff, flouncy petticoats.

'Miranda, what's wrong?' Polly suddenly broke out. 'I can't bear it—you look like someone going to her execution, not like a woman about to marry a man she loves!'

Miranda was about to say something when Aunt Ann came back with a slice of lightly buttered toast, an apple and a glass of milk. Giving her daughter a quick, suspicious look, Aunt Ann said: 'Don't hang around here, getting in our way, Polly—go and check that the other bridesmaids are ready. You'll be leaving for the church any minute.'

Polly had hesitated then given Miranda a quick kiss on the cheek. 'Be happy,' she had said and then fled with her mother's impatient eyes on her.

'Whatever you do, don't spill anything on that beautiful dress,' Aunt Ann had said, handing Miranda the plate of toast cut into bite-sized fingers. She pushed a napkin into Miranda's fingers, too. 'Don't eat too fast or you'll have indigestion. You've got plenty of time. When you've finished eating all you have to do is put on your veil.'

When she came down the stairs to meet her father, her veil had already been in place, over her pale face, and she had seen him through the floating folds of lace in a dreamlike way, his features blurred and distanced.

He had stared up at her, transfixed, and, no doubt, the ritual of the bridal gown made her appear as unfamiliar to him as she felt inside herself. The sweeping, rustling skirts forced her to move slowly, with langour, she was scarcely aware of her feet touching the ground.

Ferdy Boston had taken her hand and frowned. 'You're cold.'

She hadn't wanted to talk by then; she was anaesthetised into a blank acceptance of what was happening. If she spoke she might have to think and she did not want to do that. She hadn't paused or answered her father, she had moved on out of the door and it wasn't until they were both seated in the long, white limousine which would drive them to the church that her father spoke again.

'Still nervous, darling?'

She had shaken her head; it had been a silent lie but a necessary one, she had needed all her energy to go through with the ceremony.

'Everyone has wedding nerves,' Ferdy had soothed, patting the hand he still held. 'You shouldn't have run off, Miranda, you should have talked to me last night, told me what was in your mind. This is a big step you're taking—marriage is a serious matter. Of course, you have a few niggling little doubts, but in a week or two you'll wonder what all the fuss was about.'

'Yes,' she had said from behind her veil, her lips stiff as the word came through them, and her father hadn't said anything else, probably realising that it was wisest to leave her alone.

The last thing he had said to her, as they waited at the church door for the opening peal of the organ, had been a muttered: 'You look beautiful. Don't ever forget I love you too, and I'll always be there when you need me.'

She had pressed his arm, moved to the point of tears and unable to say anything. The music had begun and they walked down the aisle. Through her veil she had seen the dazzle of the light ahead of her and through it, Sean's black head, his long, supple back in the formal morning suit he wore. His best man glanced back at her but Sean continued to face the altar and she was grateful for that—she did not want to see his face or meet his eyes. She could only go through with this if it remained unreal, if the brittle shell of resignation surrounding her remained intact.

The moment when reality hit her was when her veil was thrust back and she saw without the clouding of the folds of lace.

Her eyes lifted and Sean stared at her, his dark eyes glittering. She had to run her nails into her palms to stop herself from turning to flee, and her pale face lost even more colour. What else could that brilliance of the eyes mean but triumph? Sean had got what he wanted, she was his wife and he was secure in his possession of her father's company from today. A sick mixture of pain and hatred welled up inside her. She could have forgiven him for using her so ruthlessly if he hadn't pretended to love her. That had been the unforgivable lie. She didn't know how she would have reacted if he had suggested an arranged marriage without pretending that he felt anything for her. She would probably have refused to listen, of course, even though she had been in love with him, but now that she knew he had been pretending all these months she felt humiliated, he had made a fool of her, coolly trapped her like a bird lured by its own driving hunger into the hunter's net.

As she signed the register later her hand felt heavy with the weight of his gold ring. She looked down as she wrote and Sean laughed softly.

'Don't forget you're Miranda Hinton now, will you?'

'As if I could,' she said and their eyes tangled. 'I'll make sure you don't,' he mocked and the other witnesses laughed although Ferdy Boston watched Miranda frowningly as he came forward to sign his own name. The immaculately cut morning suit gave him a more than usually distinguished air, his grey hair gleamed silver in the sunlight, and Miranda noticed several of the older women watching him admiringly. Ferdy still had enormous personal presence and it was not merely his wealth that made him a man women noticed. Bitterly she wondered how soon Diana would persuade him to marry her. She wished she dared tell her father everything she had overheard, but he was more than able to look after himself and her intervention might do more harm than good. It might put the idea of marrying Diana into his head when it had never previously occurred to him, and if Diana discovered later that Miranda had tried to interfere, her hostility would deepen. She might deliberately cause a breach between father and daughter, she would certainly hate Miranda more than ever.

The church was packed with familiar faces all turned towards her and Sean as they walked back down the aisle with the organ playing and the bridesmaids moving behind them, demurely holding their bouquets of spring flowers, the sweet scent of freesias so strong that it was cloying. Miranda somehow kept a smile pinned to her face, one hand through Sean's arm and the other clutching her own large bouquet. She had

chosen freesias because she loved their colour and
perfume; now she knew she would never want to
see another one of the delicate flowers for the rest
of her life. The merest trace of their perfume
would turn her stomach.

She had been so keyed up about the actual
ceremony that for a moment she had a wild rush
of relief as they emerged from the church into the
sunlight, for some reason thinking that they
would now climb back into the white limousine
and drive away. When she saw the little cluster of
men with cameras waiting outside, her heart
sank. She had forgotten that there would be
photographers present. The hand resting on
Sean's arm trembled and he looked down at her
quickly.

'All right?'

She lifted her eyes to his face and he added in a
low voice: 'Don't worry, this won't take long.'
She watched his lips move as though she had
suddenly gone deaf and had to lipread. She
wasn't really thinking about what he said,
though; she was realising that a short time ago he
had kissed her on the steps of the altar, at the
conclusion of the service. She had obediently
raised her face and his mouth had brushed over
hers but she had been too numb to feel that light
touch. Now she remembered and shivered. She
could not bear any more of this intimacy. It was
too much to ask.

Aunt Ann and Aunt Patsy began organising the
family photographs, shepherding everyone into
line, arranging people around Miranda and Sean.

People laughed and made jokes. Miranda heard herself laughing, said something in response to a question. She felt her veil blowing backwards in the spring wind. Her skirts rustled and flew upwards, she brushed them down with one hand and felt her wedding ring again. Involuntarily she twisted it around her finger, frowning down at it. She was overwhelmed with a wave of misery. This should have been the happiest day of her whole life; instead it was going to be a day she would give anything not to remember.

'Can we just have the bride and groom alone now?' one of the photographers asked.

The family drifted back and Seán and Miranda faced the cameras. Several of the photographers were from the press. One of them said jokily, 'Not so formal, Mrs Hinton!' He laughed and gave the rest of the crowd a jovial grin. 'She's forgotten her name already. Funny how weddings give brides instant amnesia, I've noticed it before.'

Miranda forced a smile which died as the man said, 'Let's have a kiss, then. This is a wedding, isn't it?'

Seán felt her tense but his own face was cool and wore a smile. He turned and put his arms round her. She didn't have time to protest or back away. He kissed her with a passion that made her eyes close on a stab of mingled pain and pleasure. She dimly heard the intake of breath from their audience, heard the cameras whirring and was vaguely aware of the flash lights. Some of her younger cousins giggled, someone else coughed and the small sounds were intrusive, they jarred and reminded her of all the things she had almost forgotten for one sweet, intolerable second.

Sean didn't look at her as he released her, she busied herself with her flyaway veil, hoping her flush wouldn't cause too much comment, praying that the photographers would finish taking their pictures soon. She still had the reception to face, heaven alone knew how many hours of smiling and pretending. She couldn't bear it. Her jaws already ached with smiling.

By the time they climbed into the white limousine she was shaking and Sean looked at her with narrowed intensity, raking back his wind-blown black hair with one hand as he turned towards her.

'You look tired. We won't have to stay at the reception for more than a couple of hours. We have to be at the airport to catch our flight by five at the latest, to check our bags through. We ought to leave the reception to change at around three-thirty. It will take us under an hour to drive to Heathrow but it's best to be on the safe side and leave ourselves plenty of time in case of traffic jams *en route*.'

She nodded, arranging her veil and tidying her hair, her eyes avoiding Sean even when she seemed to be looking in his direction. Every time he moved with the sway of the limousine she felt her nerves prickling, bitterly aware that they were alone in the car and that the driver could not hear what they said to each other although he might be able to see their reflections in his driving mirror. A frown jerked her brows together. If she found Sean's close proximity so nerve-wracking in this car, how on earth was she going to feel when they were quite alone in the villa he had borrowed from a friend? Sean had told her that the place was isolated and beautiful—perfect for a honeymoon. She had loved that idea when he first mentioned the villa in the Bahamas, now her skin went cold at the very prospect of two weeks alone with him.

How was she going to deal with this situation? How could she bear to let him touch her? This wasn't a real marriage, it was a business merger. The idea of going to bed with Sean was quite intolerable.

'Only another few hours and you can relax,' Sean said and she turned on him, barbed hostility in her voice.

'Relax? Are you kidding? It isn't so bad with other people around, I can keep pretending then—but maybe we'd better get one thing straight before we start this so-called honeymoon. You are not sleeping with me. We may be legally married, but that is as far as it goes. Lay one hand on me and I'll leave so fast you won't even see my dust.'

His smile died away and the dark eyes became glittering points of light, his lids lowered until only a slit of iris showed.

'That sounds like an ultimatum,' he said coolly.

'Oh, it is!' Miranda promised. 'And I mean it—don't think I don't.'

'Do you?' His mouth was a mocking line, she looked away from it hurriedly, her spine rigid.

'Try it and see!'

'Is that an invitation or a threat?'

'I'm not playing games, Sean,' she snapped. 'In front of other people I'll play the happy bride for you and my father, but in private you'd better keep your distance or the whole charade is over.'

The limousine slowed as they approached the house, and Sean threw a glance at the driver who was watching them curiously in his mirror. He might not be able to hear what they were saying, but their faces no doubt betrayed something of the conflict between them. Miranda tried to read Sean's expression—what was he thinking now? Was that mere irritation in his tightening mouth or a real anger? She had sounded sure of herself, confident of her ability to handle him, fierce in her determination to make him play this game by her rules for a change—but she did not make the mistake of imagining that she could force Sean to accept her terms that easily. She knew him well enough not to underestimate him. This was just a preliminary skirmish—the real fighting would come later when they were alone. She was going to have to learn to guess his intentions in advance; read every flicker passing over his face. That was where she had made her mistake in the beginning—she had fallen in love with a man she did not know. She must get to know him now, not as a lover, but as an opponent.

'I wish I knew what was behind all this,' Sean muttered. 'Something happened to you yesterday, didn't it?' His eyes probed her averted profile, relentlessly watching the rise of colour in her face. 'That's it, isn't it? Something happened between when I last saw you and when you bolted from your house.' His voice was thoughtful, sharp. 'But what on earth . . .?' He paused and she heard his breathing thicken. 'Did you meet someone at the party last night? It must be that. An old flame?'

She couldn't suppress the faint twist of her mouth which angry amusement produced and Sean noted it, frowning.

'No, obviously it isn't that, but there's something behind the way you've changed so suddenly. You met someone else? Another man?'

The limousine had parked outside the house. The chauffeur appeared at the door and opened it. Ignoring Sean, Miranda slid out of the car, her full skirts ballooning in the spring wind and her veil attempting to take off. She held it down with one hand while she moved towards the front door, where the housekeeper was waiting, all smiles.

'It was a lovely wedding, Miss Miranda, quite beautiful. I had a good cry and really enjoyed myself. What lovely flowers too, the church looked ever so nice, and the organ playing was better than usual. I'm not one for organ playing, it drones, doesn't it?' Mrs Hammond had left the church when Miranda and Sean went into the sacristy to sign the register, so that she would be back at the house in time to complete all the arrangements for the reception.

'Everything's ready, sir,' she said, looking past Miranda at Sean as he joined them. 'The caterers have been busy all morning. The marquee looks wonderful. Aren't we lucky it didn't rain? I hope that wind doesn't get any worse, we don't want the marquee blowing away half way through the lunch, do we?'

'No, we don't,' Sean agreed drily.

'Well, congratulations, sir. I hope you and Miss Miranda . . . Mrs Hinton, I should say . . . are going to be very happy.'

'Thank you.' Sean offered her his hand and she shook it, beaming broadly, her iron grey hair in newly permed curls around her flushed face. Mrs Hammond had worked for the Boston family for ten years and thought of herself as part of it. Miranda gave her a hug and got a faintly tearful smile before the housekeeper smoothed down her strawberry pink dress and clucked her tongue.

'This won't get the party organised. I'd better go and keep an eye on those caterers or half the caviar will be missing.'

The other wedding cars were already coming up the drive as the housekeeper vanished. Sean shot them a glance then said rapidly to Miranda: 'I hope for your sake that I'm wrong about you meeting someone else last night because it's too late now, Miranda. You're my wife and I'm not letting you go. We're married and we're going to have to work this out so don't start by issuing provocative ultimatums. The only result of that will be that I'll lose my temper, and you wouldn't like that, believe me.'

She was able to ignore him as the first car in the long procession halted and her father and several of her aunts got out. For the next half hour Miranda was kept busy kissing people and receiving congratulations. The wedding party was heavily weighted with her relatives; Sean's parents were both dead and he had only one brother, Declan, who was in his final year at university. A handful of distant relatives from his side had turned up at the wedding. Miranda had never met them before and they did not seem to know Sean too well, either. As she was talking to them it occurred to her that Sean was far more isolated than she had ever been. She was part of a large and closely knit family group. Sean had been in his early twenties when his parents were killed in a car crash, leaving him to take care of Declan, who had only been eleven at the time. It must have been quite a responsibility for a young man, Miranda thought, watching Sean talking to one of his second cousins.

When all the guests had arrived, Miranda and Sean joined the whole party in the marquee on one of the lawns behind the Boston home, to have lunch. Miranda could barely force herself to eat any of the delicious cold food. She picked lethargically at a plate of cold salmon in aspic and some salad, sipped a little champagne, struggled to keep smiling whenever anyone looked at her.

Once or twice she noticed Diana Cobbold who was some way down the table on which she sat. Miranda's teeth grated every time she saw the other woman. Diana was wearing an ice-blue suit whose wide lapels exposed her throat and the cleft between her breasts, making it clear that she wore no shirt underneath the suit, which was fitted so closely to her curved figure that it seemed doubtful if she could have worn anything under it anyway. She wore an enormous picture hat on her blonde head and most of the men in the marquee seemed to be watching her, too, as she vivaciously laughed and flirted with the man next to her.

Glancing at her father, who sat next to her on one side while Sean was on the other side, Miranda saw him watching Diana, too.

'That's a pretty hat Diana is wearing, isn't it?' she asked and Ferdy Boston looked round with a start.

'What? Oh, yes—she always dresses very well.'

'She's very attractive,' Miranda said, as neutrally as she could manage.

'You like her, Miranda?' Ferdy asked and Miranda wondered how to answer. Was her father asking her opinion to discover how she felt about Diana before he asked the other woman to marry him?

Carefully she said: 'I wouldn't say I liked her, no. She's not a woman's woman. She hasn't much time for her own sex—it's men's company she likes.'

Ferdy frowned, giving her a surprised stare which was puzzled and reproachful. 'She likes you.'

Miranda laughed shortly. 'Did she tell you that? Well, what a woman says and what she really thinks are two different things sometimes.'

Her father looked taken aback. 'You may be right,' he said, sounding as though she had worried him. 'I wouldn't know what goes on inside women's heads—I thought I knew you inside out, Miranda, but sometimes you even baffle me.'

She managed to laugh. 'Sometimes I baffle myself,' she said lightly, but she was being less than frank that time. All her life her father and the rest of the family had thought about her and treated her as a little girl; a cherished and spoiled little girl, her father's pet, his only heir. She had had a happy childhood, she hadn't had any of the emotional storms which often blow into someone's life in adolescence. There hadn't been any friction to cause her problems, the affection surrounding her had been too warm and understanding. Her father hadn't showered her with material gifts while neglecting her; he had always spent a good deal of time with her, she had always known she was loved.

It hadn't dawned on her until last night that, however much he loved her, he was ready to manipulate her secretly—no doubt he felt that his conspiracy was for her own good, he felt justified in what he had planned. But discovering that her father hadn't allowed her the adult freedom to make her own choices, her own decisions, had changed something inside her. Even love has no right to manipulate, to deceive, however good the intentions.

It was not so much that Miranda had grown up last night, as that she had abruptly discovered that although she was adult inside her own head, her father and Sean did not recognise the fact, but they were going to have to realise it now. Miranda had not so much changed as discovered that nobody around her had noticed that she was a mature woman, and no longer the little girl they might want her to remain.

She smiled at her father, suddenly touched. Ferdy was simply reacting the way everyone did to changes; wishing they wouldn't happen, preferring the status quo, always looking backwards to some half-remembered, half-invented golden age when problems didn't exist and life was halcyon. Time didn't stand still, though; it moved on, the relentless hand could not be halted.

'You look very distinguished in your morning suit, you should wear it more often.'

'God forbid,' Ferdy said, appalled, tugging at his stiff collar with one finger, and Miranda laughed at his expression.

A waiter appeared to take away her plate of half-eaten salmon, he gave her an indulgent smile as he noticed how little had been touched.

'Funny how brides never eat a thing,' he said, chuckling. 'They must have something else on their minds.'

Miranda caught Sean's sideways mockery and flushed, her throat closing in a new panic as she realised how soon they were going to be alone. How long would her mood of calm assurance last then?

CHAPTER FOUR

MIRANDA stood in darkness, listening, her whole body taut with a mixture of dread and excitement. She couldn't see where she was but she knew that there was someone else in the room. She heard him moving softly and strained to hear his breathing, but the heavy thud of her own heart drowned every other noise.

'You can't get away, Miranda,' he whispered, and her panic became so violent that she wanted to scream, but when she opened her mouth no sound came out. She was dumb, she could only stand and wait for him to move while she desperately tried to guess what he might do. If she kept calm she might think of a way out of the dark and suffocating room. There had to be a door—or had he locked it? Then she remembered that she had locked it herself when she came in; not realising that he was in there, waiting for her. From somewhere outside she heard a hushed murmur—was it the sea? It should have been a comforting sound, but it only increased her fear.

Suddenly she felt his hand touch her and she whirled to face him, her heart beat savage, deafening her. She saw his eyes then; bright points of light hypnotising her as she stared at them. Desire made her giddy and when he put his arms around her she was too weak to fight.

She had been waiting for this for so long, her flesh was burning, she began to kiss him, her arms going round his neck, and then he laughed softly, with triumph, and with a gasp of terror and shame she broke away, wrenching herself out of his arms, out of that heavy sleep, into a jagged awareness.

She had been dreaming. For a few seconds her relief was so enormous that she was unconscious of everything around her, then she realised that she was on the plane to the Bahamas, her perspiring body half-covered by a blanket, her seat lowered to the reclining position and Sean lying next to her, on his side, his head turned in her direction.

His eyes were open. In the dim light she saw their glitter as his head lifted. 'Can't you sleep?' he whispered.

She lay down again and pulled the blanket over her shoulders, turning on to her side with her back to him. She had no idea what time it was but it had been ten o'clock before the cabin lights were turned down and she settled to try to sleep. The day had been so exhausting, both physically and emotionally, that it hadn't taken her long to drift into a heavy oblivion.

It hadn't been difficult to maintain a polite conversation with Sean until then; from the moment they boarded the air stewardess had hovered around Sean with newspapers, drinks, cigarettes and food in an unceasing stream. She had offhandedly included Miranda in whatever offering she brought Sean, but her eyes had hardly touched on Miranda, they had been far too busy approving of Sean's looks. Quite obviously if Miranda hadn't been there Sean might have had a more personal invitation than the one the stewardess relayed from the captain; who wondered if Sean and Miranda would like to visit him and admire the auto pilot, some components of which had been made in one of Ferdy Boston's factories.

Miranda had not wanted anyone to guess that she and Sean were on their honeymoon. She had rigorously checked their hand luggage for confetti smuggled in by Declan Hinton at some stage before they left to drive to the airport. Declan had taken too many glasses of champagne during the reception; he was in a mood of wild euphoria by the time his brother and new sister-in-law drove away from the Boston home, clattering old boots and tin cans which Declan had tied on to the bumper after spraying 'Just Married' on every available inch of metal work. Luckily he had used shaving cream which Sean had managed to remove rapidly once they were out of sight of the house.

Declan had been the last to kiss Miranda before she managed to shut herself into the back of the white limousine. She had intended to give her last hug to her father, but no sooner had Ferdy stepped back to wave goodbye than long-legged, curly-haired Declan had leapt in to grab another kiss. Miranda had already seen him kissing all the bridesmaids enthusiastically a number of times. They had seemed to enjoy it as much as he did. Declan had the regular, open-faced good looks his older brother had missed His smile was infectious and his slight gawkiness charming, especially as he was good-tempered if a little crazy.

'Get your grubby paws off my bride,' Sean had commanded as he slid into the car beside Miranda and noticed the long kiss she was getting from his brother.

Declan had reluctantly released her, grinning at Sean. 'Spoilsport. Now she's my sister-in-law I get to kiss her as often as I like.'

'Try it and see what happens,' Sean said lazily stretching his long legs across the gap between the back seat and the driver's compartment 'Now, shut the door and don't drink too much champagne, when we've gone.'

Later as they were halfway to Heathrow Miranda had said: 'I'm very fond of Declan—ha he made up his mind what he wants to do when he leaves university in the summer?'

'I shudder to think. He's worked so hard thi year that once the pressure is off I won't be surprised if he breaks out and does something completely lunatic.'

'He's very lively,' Miranda had said, smiling. ' often wished I had a brother.' Her face had changed as she said that and there had been sligh bitterness in her voice as she added, 'I suppos my father did, too.'

Sean had thrown her a frowning glance, hi lean body swaying with the movement of the ca as they sped along the motorway to the airport

His dark eyes had moved from her face to the turquoise jersey silk dress she had changed into a short time ago. The smooth material clung to her, outlining the slim curve of her body, and she felt herself flushing as Sean's gaze wandered over her breasts and small waist, the soft line of her hips and the supple, silk-clad legs below the hem of her dress. That cool assessment sent her eyes skating for cover. She stared out of the window at the faintly scrubby countryside edging the road to Heathrow, her teeth gritted and a fierce sense of nervous resentment making her tense.

They had both been silent for the rest of the journey to the airport, but it had not been a calm silence—at least, Miranda hadn't felt that it was calm. The car had seemed to her to vibrate with awareness and a knife-edge apprehension.

When they were taking their seats in the first class compartment of the plane Sean's hand had brushed her breast while he was handing her a magazine and she had jerked upright as if stung by a bee, her lips parted on a silent gasp.

He had given her another of those hard, observant stares but to her relief he hadn't said anything, and once they were airborne Miranda had nervously begun to talk about Declan again. It had seemed a safe topic, one without personal overtones, and she was fond of Declan, he interested her, perhaps because he was the only close relative Sean had and the way Sean felt about his brother was some sort of clue to Sean himself. She felt she needed every clue she could unearth.

The subject of Declan had managed to occupy
them for a long time in between glasses of wine
and trays of hors d'oeuvres, followed by the
seafood salad.

'You think he'll get his degree?' Miranda had
shaken her head as the stewardess bent to offer
her another cup of coffee. 'No, thank you.'

The girl had refilled Sean's cup, smiling at him
with a little flutter of her lashes and Sean had given
her an amused smile in return, quite aware of the
girl's efforts at arousing his interest. Miranda's
mouth had stiffened and she had looked down at
the scarcely touched tray of food she had been
served. She hadn't wanted any of it but she had
pretended to be interested in it because it helped to
pass the time and keep the atmosphere between
herself and Sean stable and casual.

'Yes, I think Declan will get his degree,' Sean
had answered when the stewardess moved away.
'He's not academic, but he is intelligent, and he
has worked this year. Last year he spent far too
much time in having a good time, but for all his
recklessness and high spirits, he's too shrewd to
risk coming down without a degree to show for
three years at university.'

'It must have been hard for you to take on the
responsibility for a boy of his age when you were
so young yourself,' Miranda had said after a little
pause.

'He was my brother,' Sean said shortly. 'He
didn't have anyone else.'

'And neither did you?' she murmured with
husky sympathy.

'Obviously.' The impatience in his voice ended that conversation and she had been relieved when the cabin lights were lowered so that they could watch a film before going to sleep.

Shifting slightly on the seat, her body uncomfortably curled, Miranda tried to read her watch by the dim light in the cabin. She wasn't certain whether it was two in the morning or ten past some other hour and she didn't want to attract Sean's attention again, so she closed her eyes and tried to get back to sleep.

The white-walled villa where they were to spend the next two weeks was not visible from the road. It lay hidden among a tangle of trees, some of which bore spiky yellow flowers whose long, thin petals reminded her of the scuttling legs of yellow spiders.

She shuddered, staring at them, and Sean looked down at her quickly. 'What's wrong?'

'What on earth are those weird flowers?' she asked as the driver carried their luggage into the villa.

'Witch hazels,' he said softly, his eyes mocking her. 'Be careful they don't put a spell on you.'

'I don't believe in voodoo,' she said crossly, disliking the way he was looking at her. Now that she could see how isolated this villa was, above the beach and the dazzling blue of the sea, she felt even more nervous. She was going to be alone here with him, which made her feel like a rabbit waking up in a tiger's cage. She walked away from him into the villa before he said anything even more disturbing.

The shutters were closed over all the windows, filling the rooms with a shifting blue shadow which deepened her sense of dreamlike unreality. Miranda wandered from room to room, hearing Sean paying the driver and then the sound of the car driving away. Sean had arranged for a hire car to be delivered to the villa next day by a local firm. Miranda opened the shutters over one window and flinched away from the hot light which flooded in, realising then why someone had kept the room shuttered and cool. Glancing around she admired the pale lemon walls and the cushioned wicker furniture of the spacious sitting-room. Everything was spotless; the owner had an arrangement with a local woman who came in three times a week to do the housework.

Her nerves prickled uneasily as she heard Sean walking into the room. They were quite alone now; the pressure of that realisation made her so tense she felt her stomach clenching, but she wasn't going to let Sean see her disquiet.

Swivelling, she warily met his gaze, her eyes defiant. His mouth twisted in a faint, sardonic smile.

'I think I'll go and unpack and then have a shower,' she said, wishing she knew what was going on inside his head. He was getting some sort of warped enjoyment out of this situation, that was obvious. She might know how cold-bloodedly he had married her, but she was helpless, tied hand and foot by her own cowardice—and Sean's dark eyes were mockingly reminding her of that. She could kick herself for having gone through with the wedding: she should have cancelled it and risked the uproar which would have followed. She had chickened out of one sort of trouble only to land herself with trouble of a potentially more alarming nature.

'Why don't we go for a swim, instead?' he proposed coolly. 'There's a pool on the other side of the lawns.'

'Later, maybe,' she said, moving towards the door. 'Do you mind if I have the bedroom on this side of the house? It has a marvellous view of the sea.'

He laughed softly. 'I don't mind which bedroom we have and we'll be far too occupied to have time for admiring the view from it.'

The hair bristled on the nape of her neck. 'We're not sharing a room!'

'Oh, yes,' Sean murmured, taking off the lightweight grey jacket he wore and dropping it on a chair.

'I meant what I said to you,' Miranda said fiercely, watching with chill apprehension as he undid his tie and threw that on the chair, too. 'Legally, we may be married, but I made it quite clear to you yesterday that I wasn't sleeping with you. My self-respect wouldn't let me.' She would have been happier if she could have said that in a calm, steady voice, but Sean was now unbuttoning his shirt and Miranda nervously wondered how many more clothes he meant to remove.

'My self-respect has limits, too,' Sean said drily. 'Don't you think the maid would notice that we were sleeping apart on our honeymoon?

How long do you think it would be before she gossiped about it and it got back to the guy who lent me this place? Do you really think he'd keep such fascinating news to himself?'

'I can't help that,' Miranda muttered, hurriedly averting her eyes from him, a second too late. She wished she hadn't seen those bare, wide shoulders, that deep tanned chest with the wedge of dark hair curling up from the taut planes of his midriff. Her mouth went dry with sensual awareness, angrily she reminded herself that she must not let him get to her. She was vulnerable—he wasn't, and he would unscrupulously use her own emotions against her if she gave him the chance.

'You slept next to me last night,' Sean pointed out. 'It didn't seem to bother you, then.'

'That was different,' she said curtly. 'There were other people around.'

'You make me sound very dangerous,' Sean drawled, a wicked look in his dark eyes. 'I'm not sure whether to be flattered or insulted—what exactly do you think I'm going to do? Take you by force? I could do that now.' He took a step towards her and her pulses leaped violently. Backing, she watched him with a mixture of rage and tension.

'You may think that funny . . .' she began and his eyes narrowed.

'No, Miranda, I wasn't joking. We're quite alone here and if I seriously intended either rape or seduction, it would make little difference whether we were sharing a room or not. I don't even need a bed. I could have you here, now, on the floor, and there wouldn't be much you could do about it. I'm stronger than you are; you might fight but you couldn't stop me without having a weapon—have you got a gun in your pocket, Miranda?'

Her flush deepened and she swallowed, afraid to answer in case his softly delivered threats became a reality. He was right, of course. If he chose to take her the only way she could stop him was to kill him. She didn't have his physical strength; she couldn't fight him off.

'I'd hate you,' she whispered at last and the flash of his dark eyes made her throat close in alarm.

'I rather thought you already did,' he said with a barbed smile. 'Since you refuse to tell me why you suddenly changed your mind about me, I have to cope with the situation as it is—we're here and no way am I going to allow outsiders to gossip about us. You will sleep in the same room. There are twin beds in the room you've picked out, that will do very well. You can rest assured, I don't get turned on by a reluctant woman. You won't have to fight me off in the middle of the night.'

She stared at him, biting her inner lip. 'How do I know I can trust you to keep your word?'

His face altered, the angry amusement vanishing and his pupils hard with menace. 'You have no choice,' he bit out tersely.

She turned away, aching with a depressed realisation that he was right—she had no choice now. She had had one yesterday morning; she could have refused to go through with that wedding. By letting him stampede her into marrying him, she had blocked her own escape route. She felt like an object—she had thought she was choosing Sean but it had all been arranged for her. She had been manouevred into this marriage by two clever men; it wasn't real, any of it, but she no longer had the power of choice.

She went out of the room without looking at him again and bolted herself into the shadowy bedroom looking out over the sea which at the moment she could not see but which she heard all the time; a melancholy surge in the background as she unpacked and put away her clothes in the fitted wardrobes. When she had finished emptying the suitcases she stripped and took a shower in the glass-doored shower room leading off the bedroom.

It eased her angry tension and lowered her temperature to stand with closed eyes under the lukewarm spray of water, feeling it trickle down her back and over her breasts, washing away the perspiration of the long journey from England. She tried to think clearly but she still felt unreal, as if what was happening was a bad dream from which she couldn't wake. She was so confused. If she didn't know Sean, how could she have been in love with him? Was love merely another illusion?

Sean had been working at her father's head office for several years before Miranda met him.

She had heard her father mention him and it hadn't been difficult to guess that Ferdy Boston was impressed by Sean's ability and shrewd grasp of business, but Miranda had never been very interested in the family firm. She wasn't scientifically minded and electronics were a closed book to her, nor did she find the day-to-day workings of a company particularly riveting. She would have liked to go to art school but although she had done well at art itself, her other subjects had been rather less interesting. She hadn't achieved very high marks, and she had enough commonsense to accept that she wasn't sufficiently brilliant in art to make it her career. You had to have drive, ambition, a sense of urgent purpose, to get anywhere with a career—in art or anything else.

Sean had all those qualities, that had been obvious long before she met him. Her father recognised in Sean his own burning ambition to succeed and the way he talked about Sean had made Miranda curious about the man. She had never felt any desire to be successful, sometimes she thought it was because as a child she had been so happy. She hadn't needed to fight for the things she wanted; her father had given them to her on a plate. She had been faintly jealous of Sean, in fact, until she met him, because it had niggled her that her father thought so highly of him, and she had wondered if Ferdy Boston would have liked her to be more like that.

Sighing, she ran her hands over her wet hair, smoothing it down on her scalp, and stepped out of the shower on to the towelling mat to rub herself dry before slipping into a short robe.

Had her father and Sean planned the marriage before she ever met Sean? That idea sent a cold shiver down her spine. Barefoot, she went across the bedroom to choose something to wear. Outside, the day was languid without being hot; she wanted to stay cool for as long as possible. She was going to need to be cool if she was to cope with Sean's needling, whatever happened she had to keep her temper, not allow him to push her over the edge to some disastrous reaction.

She put on a sleeveless cotton top with a scooped neckline and a pair of bright blue satinised shorts which ended at her upper thigh, leaving a great deal of smooth bare leg exposed. Pushing her feet into cork-soled canvas beach shoes she went over to open the bedroom door a few minutes later and heard Sean whistling in the kitchen. He sounded carefree and cheerful and Miranda's teeth grated with affront at the very sound. How dare he sound so lighthearted?

She paused in the kitchen doorway. 'The bedroom is free—if you want to unpack your own cases.'

Sean was stirring a glass pitcher of iced lemonade. He looked round at her. 'Haven't you unpacked for me?' he enquired plaintively and she bared her teeth at him in a pretence of a smile.

'No, I haven't. Let's get one thing perfectly clear—I'm not here for your benefit, in any possible way. As I am here, though, I intend to enjoy a holiday, but I can manage without your company. We'll each go our own way.'

He looked at her ironically. 'If you're deliberately trying to annoy me, Miranda, you're succeeding beyond your wildest dreams. We're here for two weeks and that will give us time to talk this out—I don't intend to go back to London without having found out what the hell is behind all this, so the sooner you start talking, the easier it will be.'

'I'm going to explore the garden,' Miranda said calmly without taking any notice of his threats.

'I mean it, Miranda,' he informed her departing back but she didn't look round. His tone was charged with fury and she got a certain sort of satisfaction out of that. He had hurt her more than she could bear—she wanted to wreak some faint revenge on him, even if it was only a passing irritation.

The villa was on a smooth slope which fell down towards a silvery beach; white-capped waves rolled up on the sand and fell away with a mournful swish, and gulls and waders inhabited the otherwise empty stretch of coast. Miranda stood in the villa gardens, staring along the beach, listening to the sea and the cry of the birds. The lawns were immaculately kept and bordered by clumps of shrubs and trees beneath which were flowerbeds; a few spring flowers grew but they were unfamiliar to her. She did recognise the tulip trees, however, with their tight green buds beginning to show streaks of

white and pink as they slowly opened, and the
shiny elliptic leaves of the magnolia trees were
showing an occasional bud, too. In a few weeks
the garden would be full of the delicate white and
yellow flowers.

She wandered down a path between bougainvillaea and emerged on the beach, her appearance
making the gulls flap upwards, shrieking.
Miranda watched them, shading her eyes to
exclude the direct sunlight; their white wings
made an iridescent pattern against the blue sky,
forming arcs and arrowheads of skating light.

Smiling, her gaze lowered to the creaming
waves and caught an unexpected movement in
the shallows, a swirling and dragging object
which a closer stare suddenly told her was a man
washing in and out with the tide.

Miranda gasped and began to run down
towards him.

CHAPTER FIVE

HE seemed to be dead, his inert body lay face down in the water, and Miranda had to take a deep breath before she dared to touch him, the hair on the back of her neck lifting in a primitive fear. She pushed that aside and took the body by the waist, pulling with every ounce of strength she possessed. The man was heavy but as the tide ran in again it lifted him and helped Miranda to drag him higher up the beach, his blond hair trailing, dark with salty water, like filaments of weed.

With an effort Miranda rolled him over on to his back and knelt beside him, staring, half expecting to see some terrifying bloated corpse. His face was bronzed and ran with water, his eyelids bruised over the eyes she could not see.

Suddenly she felt sure he was not dead; she wasn't sure why, he simply looked too alive. She turned him back on to his face and began to give him artificial respiration, her body poised over his as her hands rhythmically pumped his lungs. She thought for a few seconds that it was hopeless, then she heard a faint gurgling and worked harder, with frenzied determination, until he began to cough and water poured out of him, his body shuddering and retching under her hands.

It was only as she subsided beside him, panting, perspiration running down her face, that Miranda realised what an effort she had made. She felt as if she had just run a mile.

The man lay on his face, his arms flung out, struggling with his breathing and still shivering with muscular reactions. She looked at him and tears sprang into her eyes. He looked so alive but he might so easily have been dead and he was not much older than herself. She sat with her head bowed on her knees, silently weeping in a helpless reflex of shock.

She heard movements, the man was heavily turning on to his side, lifting his head. Salt water still ran from him, his brown skin glistened with it. She ran a trembling hand over her wet eyes, sniffing like a little girl.

'Thanks,' the man said. His eyes were open now; bright blue between wet lashes. He was breathing less raggedly, but his voice was hoarse.

'How do you feel?' Miranda asked.

'Sick,' he said, but he grinned.

Miranda turned and stared out to sea; there was no sign of a boat. How had he got there? When she was standing on the villa lawn she had noticed that there were no footprints on the beach; the sand was virgin and blank apart from the faint, triangular prints of birds' feet close to the water's edge.

'How did you get here?' she asked. 'Were you sailing?'

'Windsurfing,' he said. 'From Jago Beach— around that headland there! I went further than

I'd meant to and the wind drove me on to the rocks. I didn't even see them, they're just below the surface. The first I knew was when the board crashed upwards. I was thrown right up in the air. I only had one option—to swim for shore.'

Miranda stood up and peered towards the headland marking the end of the beach. She thought she saw a red sail washing backwards and forwards on the waves, but it seemed to be far away. If he had swum that distance he must have been exhausted.

'You saved my life,' he said, slowly sitting up. Holding out a hand he said: 'I'm Marty Knox, by the way.'

'Miranda Boston,' she said and then realised she had given her maiden name but it was too late to correct it, she began to flush at the very idea of admitting that she was on her honeymoon.

His laughter was spontaneous. 'How apt,' he said, but she didn't get the point and stared, sitting down again beside him.

'Sorry?'

'Never mind,' he said. 'Do you live here, Miranda?'

'I'm staying here—up there.' Her head jerked towards the villa. 'Do you live on the island?'

'I'm on holiday here, too. I live in Saudi Arabia—I'm an engineer working on a government project over there. I've been there two years and I've got a long leave owing.' He broke off, breathing thickly. 'God, I feel rotten,' he muttered, his head bent, the blond hair hanging damply over his forehead.

'You'd better come up to the villa and we'll ring for a doctor,' Miranda suggested, getting to her feet. 'Let me help you,' she added quickly as he struggled to get up too. She put an arm around his waist and he managed to get to his feet. He was slim but muscular, when he leaned on her shoulder the weight surprised her.

'We'll take it slowly,' she promised as she felt the tremor run through his body, after a few steps.

He turned his head and looked down at her, his blue eyes smiling. 'Thank the lord you were on that beach. If you hadn't been, I'd be dead.'

'Don't be morbid,' she said, feeling his arm going round her waist to steady him as he took another step, his body swaying. 'Are you okay?' she asked quickly and he nodded.

It took them a long time to negotiate the climb back up to the villa gardens and Marty was breathing in sharp, jagged bursts as they made it. He paused among the magnolia trees, a hand to his chest, his head hanging. Miranda watched him anxiously.

He lifted his head as his breathing eased and smiled at her ruefully. 'Sorry about this.'

'Don't be silly,' she chided. 'Of course you're breathless—what do you expect?'

He leaned down and kissed her lightly on the lips, both arms round her. 'You're a honey,' he whispered, then grimaced at her. 'Well, let's get this show on the road or we might never make it.'

As they turned back to face the villa, Sean appeared on the veranda running along the back of the building. He leaned on the white-painted rail, his long body casually posed, watching them, but even at that distance Miranda was aware of a hidden anger behind his cool expression. The black eyes glittered, the mouth was taut with control. Sean obviously did not like the intrusion of a stranger into their secluded villa.

Marty saw him, too, and stared. Looking at Miranda he asked quizzically: 'Hey, who's that?'

'My husband,' she reluctantly admitted and saw surprise in Marty's face—and something else, a brief disappointment. Or was she imagining that? It was gone before she could be sure.

'I hope he didn't see me kiss you,' he wryly muttered. 'He might have wondered what was going on, is he the jealous type?'

Miranda didn't answer; the question was too complex. How did she know what type Sean was? But she couldn't admit that, could she?

Sean strolled to meet them, his body blocking the steps up to the veranda, his face a cool, antagonistic mask from which the dark eyes watched her with a menace she hoped Marty could not read.

'Your wife just saved my life,' Marty said in his salt-roughened voice, smiling at Sean whose face didn't alter by an inch, the planes of it angular and cold.

Miranda hurriedly plunged into speech too. 'Mr Knox was windsurfing and ran into some rocks. He was almost drowned. I found him on the beach.'

'I'd just made it to the beach when I must have passed out,' said Marty. 'When I came to I was on my face and your wife was pumping me out.' He grinned at Sean again. 'She's wonderful,' he added, a compliment Sean registered by lifting his brows slightly.

'I should think you need a drink,' Sean drawled. His glance touched on Miranda. 'Both of you,' he added, leaving a curious impression of menace on the air. Marty gave her a bewildered look, she looked away without showing anything. Sean was being distinctly inhospitable and she was embarrassed.

Sean led the way into the villa and Marty paused, grimacing, as he looked down at the damp patches he was leaving on the parquet floor. 'I'm afraid I'm still very wet.'

'I'll get you a towel,' Miranda offered, darting away to hunt for one in the bathroom.

When she got back Marty was talking nervously, his gaze apprehensive as it watched Sean's hard face. 'I've been here a week, I've got another week here and then I go home to England for the rest of my leave, I'm looking forward to seeing my family again, I can tell you.' He looked round in relief as Miranda re-appeared with the towel. 'If it wasn't for your wife, I might never have seen them again,' he added, smiling at her.

'If I were you, I'd avoid dangerous sports for the next week,' Sean said drily and Miranda gave him a quick, suspicious look, hearing an undertone. He met her look blandly. 'What would you like to drink?' he added.

Miranda handed Marty the towel as he said, 'I'd love a whisky and ginger, if you have it, Mr Boston.'

Sean did a double-take, staring. Marty was unaware of it, he was too busy towelling himself dry. Miranda felt herself flushing as she met Sean's narrowed, comprehending eyes—there was still anger in them, the lustrous black pupils were glazed with temper, but he didn't inform Marty that she had given the wrong name or make any verbal comment on her slip apart from that one, hard, sardonic stare.

Miranda had brought one of Sean's towelling robes with her from the bathroom. She handed it to Marty as he finished drying his feet, and he grinned gratefully at her.

'You think of everything, thanks. I'll feel quite human now.' He slipped into the robe and tied the belt, then sat down at Sean's gesture of invitation on one of the wicker chairs, the cane creaking at his weight. 'I'm sorry to have caused all this trouble, Mr Boston,' he said to Sean, accepting the glass held out to him. He held it between both hands, his bronzed skin still carrying an undercoat of pallor after his close brush with death, his blond hair paler now that it was dry. He was a very good-looking man apparently in his twenties; obviously athletic and very fit.

Sean came over to give Miranda her own glass of brandy, his cool fingers touched her hand as he gave the glass to her and she hurriedly backed away to sit down, nervously conscious of Sean's appraising stare as she did so.

Marty was looking around the room curiously. 'Nice place here—you're renting it, I gather? If you've got company a rented place is fun, more privacy; you can do more or less as you like, I suppose. Not being married, I prefer hotels; you get a chance to meet people. More scope for holiday romance.' He grinned at Miranda, who smiled back.

'You're looking for holiday romance, are you?' Sean murmured, watching them both.

Marty drank his whisky, slightly flustered by Sean's level gaze, and Miranda gave Sean an angry glare. Even Marty was picking up the barbed nuances of Sean's comments now; it was embarrassing.

Marty finished his drink and put down the glass. 'Well, thanks again for saving my life,' he said as he got up. 'I ought to be getting back to my hotel—if you've got a 'phone perhaps you'd be good enough to let me use it to ring them and ask them to send a car to pick me up?'

'By all means,' Sean said, and Miranda swallowed her brandy, the heat of the spirits making her shudder, then got up and collected the wet, sandy towel which Marty had used and took it off to the kitchen where she dropped it into the washing basket. She heard Marty talking on the 'phone in the lounge as she went into the bedroom a moment later.

Her own clothes were wet and sand-stained. She bolted the door and stripped off rapidly to take another shower, her skin was gritty with sand. When she had dried herself she put on clean clothes; pale pink cotton pants and a blue sleeveless top, striped with white. She brushed her dark brown hair and added a touch of lipstick before she went back to the lounge.

Marty and Sean were talking politely about Saudi Arabia. They had glasses in their hands, each containing a finger of whisky and a couple of pieces of ice. Sean swirled his glass while Marty was saying: 'Can't drink out there, of course; not that that bothers me much because I'm not a great drinker normally. I'm a social drinker; parties and people's houses but not when I'm alone. I can take it or leave it, but it bothers some of the guys out there. It's the heat and the flies that I can't stand, but you get used to it, and the money is good.' He halted as Miranda joined them and smiled cheerfully at her. 'You look very cool and collected.' His eyes admired the pink pants and brief top, and, with Sean watching them, Miranda felt herself flushing.

'Thank you, I had a shower. Is your hotel sending a car?'

'Should be here any minute,' he nodded, and drank some whisky. 'Look, I feel I owe you something special—will you have dinner with me one evening?' He looked quickly at Sean, 'Both of you, of course.'

Sean looked impassively at Miranda before answering 'We'll take a rain-check on that, shall we? We only arrived today and we haven't had a chance to settle in here yet. Some other time, but thank you for the invitation.'

Miranda looked out of the window at the

halcyon sky, watching the deep amber glow of the
sun as it began to descend. The evening was
about to fall; she was going to be alone here with
Sean and that thought made her intensely
nervous. In the silence they all heard the sound
of a car engine and Marty gave a faint sigh.

'That will be from the hotel,' he said, putting
down his glass. He turned to Miranda, offering
his hand. 'I'll never be able to thank you enough.'

'Nonsense,' she stammered, rather pink. 'I
only did what anyone would have done.'

He smiled wryly. 'But it wasn't just anyone—it
was you who saved me and that makes you very
special.' He lifted her hand to his lips before she
realised what he meant to do and brushed a kiss
on the back of her hand. She felt her flush deeper
dramatically and agitatedly pulled her fingers
free, avoiding the lance of Sean's watchful stare.
He hadn't liked that; he was taut and immobile
beside her but for all his stillness she felt his
anger. He might not be in love with her himself
but he was a man to whom possession meant a
great deal. That was why he was so determined to
have her father's company; his hunger for power
involved a desire for submission in the objects he
chose to acquire. Possession is only complete
when all resistance ceases. Sean resented other
men coming near her.

They walked to the door in an uneasy silence.
Marty watched them out of the corner of his eyes,
frowning. He paused at the front door and held
out his hand to Sean. 'I forgot to thank you, too,
Mr Boston, for your hospitality.' His voice was

formal and his expression cool. He liked Sean no more than Sean liked him.

'Not at all,' Sean said shortly.

Marty walked towards the estate car which had pulled up outside the villa. It bore the hotel's name blazoned across one side. Marty stopped to look back before he got into the car, waving. 'See you soon, I hope!' The message was for Miranda, his eyes didn't even touch Sean.

Miranda waved back and watched the vehicle turn and carefully negotiate the driveway past the scraping branches of the witch hazels, then she turned and went back into the villa with Sean on her heels. She was intensely nervous but she was determined not to show it. Attack was supposed to be the best method of defence so she turned on him as they walked into the lounge, her blue eyes spitting defiance.

'Did you have to be so offhand? Marty had just been through a terrifying experience that left him shattered!' she accused.

His lip curled back in a barbed smile. 'It left him fancying the brave little heroine who snatched him from a watery grave!'

She struggled to control the rush of colour invading her face. 'Don't be absurd! He was grateful to me, that's all.'

'You only met him half an hour ago, yet he kissed you as you came up the garden and then kissed your hand when he was leaving—fast work for a half-drowned man. I shudder to think how quickly he can work when he's normal.'

Her eyes lowered briefly. 'I thought he was a

pleasant, friendly man and you're building him up into some sort of Don Juan!'

Sean caught her shoulders in a punishing grip and she looked up again, her face agitated. 'You gave him your maiden name, didn't you?' he demanded.

'I was off balance,' she stammered. 'I forgot.'

'Don't ever forget you're married to me again, do you hear?' He shook her and she struggled to break free, her slim body writhing helplessly.

'There's no need to make such a fuss about a simple slip of the tongue!'

'A Freudian slip,' Sean said tersely. 'You meet an attractive guy and conveniently forget you're married. Well, you may want to forget that you're my wife but I'm not going to let you, Miranda.'

The dangerous dark eyes stared down into her own, all the bones in his face locked in bitter tension, and Miranda was suddenly deeply afraid of him, of a threat she read in his stare and the poised menace of his supple body. She had realised that Sean was angry, that he resented Marty Knox's appearance in their lives, but she hadn't suspected that his rage was so fierce.

'Get your hands off me,' she began, her fear becoming a burning resentment which showed in her bitter blue eyes, but she wasn't given a chance to finish that sentence because Sean put his head down and crushed the next words back into her parted mouth. She couldn't breathe, his kiss suffocating and insistent, his arm going round her to force her body against his own. Miranda hated that kiss, she fought it with every nerve, her body struggling uselessly, and then Sean changed his tactics. His mouth lifted for a second and as she snatched a hoarse breath it came down again with a very different intention; his lips moulding hers softly, in heated sensuality.

Her eyes shut weakly, her mouth moved hungrily against his, and Sean's hand slid under her top and sleekly caressed her bare midriff, crept up to touch her breasts with an intimacy that made her nipples harden with an inflow of blood. Miranda forgot everything for one mindless moment; her spine arching in an involuntary spasm of desire.

For some inexplicable reason she suddenly remembered the first time he ever kissed her, on the night of their first date. They had sat talking in his car for some time and Miranda had kept wondering if he would kiss her, she had kept watching his mouth move and feeling her insides turn to water at the very idea of Sean kissing her with that firm, very masculine mouth. Sean had stopped talking and she hadn't even realised it for a moment, her eyes had been riveted on his lips. They had curved into an amused smile and then she had looked up, startled and flushed at having been caught watching him like that. Then he had leaned forward and with a breathless gasp she had leaned forward too, very shaky and excited, and as he kissed her she had closed her eyes. Somehow that kiss had not been the way she had expected it, the way she had anticipated it in her mind. Sean had been gentle, almost indulgent, he hadn't kissed her with the insistent demand he was making now.

She frowned, stiffening in his arms. Was he acting? Was this passion only another way of manipulating her? Stung, she pushed him away, almost reeling backwards as Sean released her while she was struggling with him.

'You bastard!' she stammered, her colour hectic. 'Keep your hands off me or I'll fly straight back to England.'

Sean stared, a tiny muscle flickering beside his mouth. He was even more flushed than she was; his cheekbones stained with dark red. She heard his ragged breathing, his chest rose and fell rapidly as he dragged air into his lungs.

'You wanted me,' he said unsteadily, his dark eyes glittering with aroused excitement, and Miranda's ears rang with a wild beat. She couldn't deny it but that wasn't what made her heart hammer—she saw Sean off balance for the first time in her memory, he was out of control. He might have begun to make love to her from temper, but other, more physical, reactions had taken over a moment later.

'Don't kid yourself,' she said angrily. She wasn't going to let him imagine that he had got to her; if he was off balance she wanted to keep him that way.

Sometimes when Sean kissed her she had felt like someone driving a car who puts a foot down on the accelerator and feels no immediate leap of power in response, only a dull note. She had never felt that Sean wanted her with the same hungry need she felt for him; he had never lost his head or answered her passion with an equal desire. He had kept the fire of their lovemaking damped down until now.

She was puzzled by the change in him. Had her resistance been the spark which ignited feelings of which Sean had been either unaware or unwilling to admit? Was his desire the outward expression of possessive instincts she was thwarting? Or had it been the appearance of another man—even a polite stranger—on the scene which had made him jealous and inspired in him this violent rage for possession?

But how could she be sure what was going on inside him, when she really didn't know him at all?

'I'm not the one who's deluded, Miranda,' he said grimly. 'It's you who has a problem knowing what she wants.'

'I know I don't want this farce of a marriage,' Miranda muttered, turning away. 'It isn't real!' He took her shoulder and spun her round to face him again.

'I can make it very real,' Sean said, and she bit her lip at the mocking intimacy of his voice. 'Any time you like,' he added softly.

'Can you make me free again?' she threw at him.

She felt him stiffen. 'A week ago . . .' he began but she couldn't let him finish that sentence.

'A week ago I hadn't had my eyes opened,' she interrupted angrily.

'Who by?' he demanded at once. 'About what?

For heaven's sake, will you tell me what you accuse me of? We dated for six months before we were married. I thought you wanted this marriage as much as I did.'

'But not for the same reasons,' she said, and he stared at her, the dark eyes penetrating as they tried to probe the pale planes of her face.

'What were your reasons?' he asked at last. 'Are you saying that you never loved me?'

'I'm saying that you wanted to marry me because you knew that if you did, you would get control of my father's company,' Miranda said flatly. 'Don't deny it now—I told you that on our wedding day and you didn't deny it then, so please, don't start lying again now.'

'You were hysterical on our wedding day, I didn't think you knew what you were saying and I wasn't sure what had triggered off your sudden panic,' Sean said impatiently. 'God knows where you got the idea that I was admitting that I was only marrying you for the company. I can't have said anything of the kind. You've put words into my mouth.'

Miranda laughed bitterly. 'Please, spare me a long denial! I know you and my father discussed the settlement even before you proposed to me.'

Sean's eyes narrowed. 'You know? Did Ferdy tell you?'

She met his stare ironically. 'Does it matter who told me? You're tacitly admitting that it's the truth—and don't hurriedly start denying it again, because I'm not as big a fool as you seem to think. You may have deceived me once, but you never will again.'

She moved to the door in the charged silence that followed. 'I'm going to see what food there is in the kitchen,' she said as she went out and Sean did not even answer her.

CHAPTER SIX

THE maid who looked after the villa during the owner's absence had left the kitchen well stocked with food; fresh, frozen and canned. Miranda found a selection of salad vegetables in the lowest compartment of the fridge and on a higher shelf she discovered some prepared crabs. She mixed a salad, laid the table in the dining alcove which opened off the kitchen, and called Sean.

He eyed the crabs suspiciously. 'Are they fresh, do you think? Shell fish can be very dicey.'

'The maid left a note saying they were caught this morning,' Miranda told him, producing it.

'Okay, we'll risk it.' Sean wandered over to the table and stared out of the window beside it at the darkened garden. The sea beyond was as flat as a mill pond; a huge silver moon was laying a glittering patina on the quiet surface of the water.

Miranda carried the bowl of salad to the table and went back for the crabs. 'You could open the wine,' she told Sean over her shoulder.

'Corkscrew?' he asked.

'Try that drawer there, it appears to be where the maid keeps odd utensils. She's very methodical, everything has a place.'

Sean found the corkscrew and opened the bottle of white wine which Miranda had unearthed in the bottom of the fridge; a misty film on the dark glass bottle.

As she sat down Sean poured her a glass of wine, his body supple as he leaned across to do so. Miranda helped herself to salad.

'I'm not sure about some of these ingredients—I've never seen that yellow thing before, it looks like a shrivelled parsnip.'

Sean laughed. 'What matters is how it tastes.'

They both tasted the yellow vegetable, which Miranda had grated; it was sweet and not unlike potato. 'I think I should have cooked it,' Miranda said. 'But you learn by experience.'

'Yes,' Sean said drily, giving her a mocking smile.

Miranda ignored that, concentrating on her meal. The wine made her sleepier; she started to yawn as they were drinking the coffee which Sean had made, and he said, 'Why don't you get off to bed? I'll clear the table and wash up.'

She was surprised by the offer but accepted with alacrity. If they were to share a bedroom she would prefer to get into bed before he appeared. She finished her coffee and stood up, slightly flushed as she met his cool stare.

'Well, I'll . . .' her voice trailed away at the amusement in his face and she turned and walked out quickly to get away before she lost her temper. Sean might find this funny, but she did not.

In the bedroom she hurriedly undressed and dived into one of the twin beds, switching out the light only a few moments later. She did not imagine she would get to sleep before Sean appeared, but in fact he didn't hurry and she slowly fell asleep while she listened for the sounds of his footsteps.

When she woke up she was still alone although a quick glance at the other bed showed her that Sean had slept in it last night; the sheet was thrown back and the bed rumpled, the pillow still bore the imprint of his head.

She listened intently—was he in the shower room? No sound of splashing reached her so she rapidly leapt out of bed and grabbed a towelling robe to sprint into the shower. The cool water woke her up properly. Slicking back her wet hair she put on the robe and went back into the bedroom. It was still empty but as she went towards the door to bolt it before getting dressed, it opened and Sean halted, staring at her.

'Oh, you're up!' He had a cup of coffee in his hand and offered it to her. He was wearing a white cotton tracksuit and trainer shoes and looked flushed.

'You haven't been jogging?' Miranda asked in surprise. She knew he kept fit with running and frequent visits to the gym when he was in London but she hadn't expected him to jog here in this heat.

'Along the beach,' he nodded, his eyes wandering over her and she self-consciously remembered that she was naked under the short robe. Turning away quickly she sipped the coffee, as Sean added, 'I have to use up my spare energy somehow.'

There was mockery implied in that remark so she ignored it. 'I was just going to get dressed,' she said pointedly.

Sean sat down on his own bed.

Miranda shot him an angry look. 'I don't want an audience.'

'Drink your coffee while it's hot,' he drawled, showing no sign of moving. 'I want to talk to you and now is as good a time as any.'

'What about?' She sat down, carefully pulling the hem of her robe together and covering her knees with it, while Sean watched sarcastically.

'I thought we might spend most of the day on the beach, is that okay with you? We could both use a break to wind down.'

'That sounds fine.' She drank some more coffee. 'Have you eaten yet?'

'No, I just had a cup of coffee, but I'm hungry.'

'When I'm dressed, I'll make breakfast then,' said Miranda, putting down her empty cup.

Sean stood up and pulled the top of his tracksuit over his head. She stiffened, instantly apprehensive, and he eyed her ironically. 'I'm going to take a shower.' He walked towards the shower room, his bare brown shoulders rippling with muscle and the graceful line of his spine riveting her eyes. She could see a scattering of fine dark hair on his back but his skin was deeply tanned.

As the glass door closed Miranda went to the wardrobe and found a bikini and a large square of flower-printed gauze. She threw off her robe and put on the bikini, tying the gauze around her body as a sarong, then left the room to prepare some breakfast. Sean joined her ten minutes later. He had put on black swimming trunks over which he wore an open towelling robe. His hair was damp and he had shaved. Miranda had put a bowl of fruit in the centre of the table and sliced some of the dome-shaped bread she had found in a breadbin. Fresh coffee steamed in a pot.

Sean sat down and picked up a piece of bread, spreading it with some marmalade. Miranda sat opposite, pouring the coffee. It struck her suddenly that this was how she had imagined their honeymoon; the two of them together in a quiet, sunlit place doing ordinary things together, having meals, talking, sunbathing and swimming. She had had a glowing image which from outside might now seem to be coming true—the reality was bitterly different.

'Why the sigh?' Sean asked probingly, looking up.

She passed him his cup. 'Did I sigh? I wasn't aware of it.'

'You never answer a straight question,' Sean muttered impatiently. 'Why can't you talk to me? What am I supposed to do—read your mind? I wish to God I could.'

'Maybe it's as well you can't,' she said and heard his intake of breath.

'What's that supposed to mean?'

'Work it out for yourself.' She deliberately did not look at his lean figure opposite her; she didn't need to look, she knew precisely how he looked, that image was imprinted on her mind. Her skin prickled with awareness whenever he was in the same room as her.

'Stop talking in riddles,' he grated, leaning towards her with violence implicit in the tense movement. 'What were you thinking that I wouldn't like if I knew about it?'

She shrugged and he bit out, 'Another man?'

Miranda laughed involuntarily, it was so ironic that he should keep harping on the idea that she was interested in another man when she had more than enough problems coping with him. She wasn't going to tell him that, of course. Why should she give him even the vaguest clue that no other man could ever do a thing to her pulse rate? Sean must never know how passionately she loved him; he would only use the information against her.

'What's funny?' Sean asked curtly, his eyes fixed on her as if he wished he could lift up the top of her head and have a bird's eye view of the workings of her mind. Yes, no doubt he would like to read her mind, but she was deeply relieved that he couldn't.

'Who is it?' he asked in the same terse voice.

'Who's what?' she asked, eyes deliberately wide and blank.

'Don't give me that innocent look—you know who I mean! There has to be somebody, you wouldn't just lose interest in me overnight unless there was a counter attraction.'

'Your trouble is, you don't listen,' she said, getting up, as she finished her coffee. 'I'm not

very hungry this morning, I think I'll take some
fruit down to the beach. It will taste better in the
sunshine.'

'I'm getting pretty sick of the way you change
the subject every time I try to find out what went
wrong between us,' Sean said forcefully, watching
her walk out.

While they were walking down to the beach
later he suddenly asked; 'How long were you at
Clare Holm's flat that night?'

Puzzled, she hesitated, wondering what lay
behind that question. In the end she said, 'I can't
remember—why?'

'Did you go straight there—or did you take a
detour *en route*?'

Light dawned and Miranda almost laughed
again, but his tone was terse enough now, so she
simply shrugged. 'I don't know what you're
getting at.'

'You aren't stupid!' he exploded and she
turned her head to give him a sweet smile.

'Thanks, how kind.'

Her mockery didn't soothe the savage beast, he
glowered, his lip curling back from his teeth.
'Did you go somewhere else before you went to
that woman's flat? Who else did you go to see?'

She looked sideways and saw the jut of his
chin, the angular edge of his profile. He had the
stubborn, tenacious air of a man determined to
get answers and Miranda felt an odd dart of
tenderness, but hurriedly looked away as he
turned to meet her gaze. Whatever happened she
must not weaken. She had Sean's full attention—

for the first time since they met. She wasn't going to be stupid enough to lose it. She had seen him constantly during the past six months, but she had never felt he really saw her. Sean was a hectically busy, preoccupied man whose leisure hours were few, fitted in between more important business. His mind was often, she had secretly suspected, on something else; when they were having dinner he would occasionally lapse into an abstracted silence and when she spoke would look up with a startled expression as if having forgotten she was there.

Well, he was really seeing her now, she could be sure he wasn't taking her for granted any more. How many times had she felt, even when he was kissing her, that he had something more vital on his mind? It was very offputting to kiss a man who looked at you vaguely a moment later, as if wondering who you were. If he kissed her now, at least, she could be sure he wasn't going through the motions while half-poised, eager to get back to work.

Until he actually asked her to marry him she had thought from time to time that she was going to lose him, that he would stop asking her for dates. She had been so uncertain of him, puzzled and tense with frustration, afraid to let her own urgent feelings show in case he rejected them. Women were so helpless in such a situation; making the first move, taking the initiative, might be thought modern but most men did not have modern minds, they wanted to be the ones who chased not the ones who were pursued, they wanted to be the hunter not the prey, and Miranda had known instinctively that with Sean she would have to wait until he showed her how he felt.

Even his proposal had hardly been romantic—he had been flying to Hamburg and she had had lunch with him first, hating the idea of not seeing him for four days and snatching at every last minute before he had to leave. He had kissed her before getting into the waiting car, looked down at her and said, 'Will you marry me, Miranda? Think about it while I'm gone.'

She hadn't had a chance to answer, he had got into the car and while she was still breathless had driven away. For a stupid minute or two she had wanted to run after the car, shouting: 'Yes, yes, please,' and joy had fountained inside her, making her laugh like a crazy fool while she stood there in the street with passers-by staring at her warily. She hadn't come down from that wild height for hours and then she had begun to wonder again, to question, to doubt. Sean wouldn't have asked her to marry him if he hadn't loved her, but she wished he had proposed in some other way, not flung the question briskly at her in a street and then driven off as though he had simply asked her for another date. She had see-sawed for the next four days between happiness and uncertainty, but when she saw Sean again and he gave her that intimate smile which she wanted so badly to believe no other woman had ever seen, asking: 'Made up your mind yet? Are you going to marry me?' she had gone blindly into his arms with her whispered: 'Yes,' and put aside all her questions. That had not stifled them; they had returned, like the sea leaping back up this beach, every time she kissed him without getting the response she ached for.

Yesterday he had kissed her angrily. She had hated it, but at least she had known his emotion was totally real and held a power his kiss had never held in the past, and a few minutes later it had suffered a sea-change into something else. For the first time Sean had kissed her with a desire which was urgent, and Miranda had immediately known the difference. How could you miss it, she thought? It was the difference between the real and the false nightingale in the fairy story.

They emerged from the massed bougainvillaea on to white sand stretching in untrodden smoothness except where the red-legged waders advanced along the tide's edge, bowing their heads to peer downwards as they scuttled through the surf, like a hurrying army of office cleaners sweeping everything they saw out of sight.

Miranda wandered down, surveying the beach for the best spot to spread her towel. The sun was not yet too hot, the breeze kept the temperature down. Sean watched her, his hands on his lean hips, his black hair blowing back from his face.

She finally settled on a part of the beach well above the rising tide and spread her towel, sitting on it to smooth suntan lotion into her skin, while Sean lay next to her, sunglasses hiding his eyes from her. He appeared to be asleep but she suspected him of watching her; the lenses of his glasses flashed in the sun making it impossible for her to be sure. Below them his features were relaxed and calm; his brown skin glistening, his mouth a warm, parted line.

Miranda slept on and off during the morning. Each time she woke with a start, drowsy and sunflushed, to hear the idyllic sounds of the beach all around her—the shrill cry of the gulls, the swish of the waves, the rustle of the leaves in the villa gardens.

Once she ate some fruit and later drank some mineral water she had brought down to the beach in her basket. Sean had sat up each time and accepted what she offered. She kept her eyes averted from the lean strength of his body but she was permanently aware of its proximity and her own physical reactions. Desire ignored the reasoning of the mind, like a wild animal on a leash it refused restraint and struggled all the time to escape. To take her mind off the subject obsessing it, she decided to swim and got up; tying back her dark hair while Sean watched her. She ran down the hot sand, hearing him coming after her, and waded into the water with a sensation of relief at the coolness on her sunwarmed skin.

As she swam away from the shore she heard Sean moving behind her, his long arms cutting through the waves in a regular rhythm. The blue surface of the sea glittered with sunlight, dazzling her, and she turned back to face the shore, floating on the swell of the sea, staring at the white-walled villa set among its green gardens.

'Race you back!' Sean challenged a few minutes later, his black head emerging from the waves like the head of a seal, and Miranda laughed and dived away, swimming strongly for the shore.

Sean passed her just before she reached the shallows and as her feet touched the shifting sand she saw him waiting for her; legs apart, his tanned body gleaming in the sunlight, laughter in his face and the glitter of triumph.

'You like to win, don't you?' she said coolly, eyeing him.

'Doesn't everyone?'

'Not everyone is so competitive.'

His smile died. 'Is that something else you don't like about me?'

Miranda waded through the shallow water without answering and Sean's hand shot out to grab her and spin her to face him. She stumbled and he caught her in his arms, their wet bodies sliding against one another. Instinctively she clutched at his bare shoulders and Sean's mouth came down in an oddly searching movement to which she offered no resistance, at first, her limbs heavy and languorous as she yielded to that kiss. That first reaction only lasted for a moment, then her mind screamed a denial and she started to fight him off. She knew she must not give in to her need for him; Sean must not have a walk-over with her or she was lost.

When she struggled and pushed at his shoulders she felt him tense and the coaxing kiss grew harder, almost brutal, forcing her lips to yield with a savage determination which made her angrier. Her hands curled into fists and beat on his chest, she kicked his calves and writhed in his hands, but her own violence was a mistake because it made her slip again and this time Sean did not try to halt her fall, he let go of her and watched her sprawl into the water at his feet.

Before she could scramble to her feet again, he threw himself down on her, pinning her shoulders to the sand, her hair floating on the rising and falling tide and her eyes wide with shock as they stared at him. He didn't say anything, he was breathing roughly, thickly; his face flushed darkly and his eyes glazed with an emotion she recognised with a shudder. No one had ever looked at her like that before, but her female instincts recognised that look all the same, and her ability to think clearly deserted her.

Sean's mouth hurt; he meant it to, she realised, struggling weakly underneath him, her hands grabbing his wet hair and tugging it in a vain attempt to stop him. His hands explored her body while his knees pinioned her, she couldn't turn her head away from the angry force of his mouth because she was pillowed in water, it ran into her ears and surged through her hair. Sean slid a hand under her and unhooked her bikini top, dragging it off a moment later. Out of the corner of one eye she saw it floating away on the tide, a tiny scrap of bright material.

She didn't know she was screaming, but his mouth silenced the sound just as she realised that he shrill cries of panic came from herself. He was touching her wet bare breasts, his knee nudging her thighs apart, and desperation gave her a new charge of strength. She bucked like a terrified mare, running her nails into his back, and Sean lifted his head, grunting in pain, sprawling sideways and giving her a chance to scramble to her feet at last.

She ran, sobbing, her hands across her naked body. Behind her she heard him splashing to his feet and fear was a spur, she put on more speed, her breath coming hoarsely from her lungs.

Sean caught up with her among the glossy-leaved magnolia trees. As his arms grabbed her she began to shake, trying to fight him off, and he held her tightly, his head bent over her. 'I'm sorry,' he muttered, his voice breathless. His cheek gently rubbed backwards and forwards on the wet strands of her hair and she heard the difference in his voice and stopped struggling, her legs weak under her. 'I went a little crazy, that was stupid of me, I'm sorry,' he said.

She began to cry again and heard him swear. 'Miranda,' he whispered, his arms tightening on her shuddering body. She could hardly stand, shock made her so weak, her teeth were chattering and she was white. Sean suddenly lifted her off her feet and carried her into the villa. He walked into their bedroom and put her down on the bed, wrapped a duvet around her and knelt beside her, gently massaging her body under the duvet, his hands rubbing up and down her arms and shoulders.

She kept her eyes shut, afraid to look at him Slowly the trembling ceased and warmth begar to percolate through her limbs. Sean left her or the bed and went out in silence and she lay there so dazed that she couldn't even think. A few moments later Sean returned with a cup of milky coffee. He lifted her up, an arm around her shoulders, and put the cup to her lips. She swallowed, grimacing.

'What . . .'

'Brandy,' Sean said tersely. 'Drink it, I only put a dash into the coffee.'

She drank some more, her eyes down, lashes flickering on her pale cheeks. She felt him watching her and risked a quick glance at him through her lashes; he was pale, too, under his tan, and his eyes were grim. He took the cup away and she sat huddled in the duvet, watching him.

With his back to her, he said: 'I would have sworn I wasn't capable of something like that—I suppose you never expect primitive instincts in yourself. Saying that I'm sorry isn't much use, is it? I'm sorry it happened, I haven't any excuse for myself, but it won't happen again, you needn't be afraid of that. I'd never have behaved like that if you hadn't made me blind with rage . . .'

'Hang on,' Miranda interrupted angrily. 'A minute ago you said you had no excuse—what are you saying now? That it was my fault?'

'No, of course not,' he said shifting restlessly. 'But if you . . .'

'I asked for it, I suppose?' she broke in furiously and his frown carved a deep furrow across his temples.

'Don't put words into my mouth, Miranda. I'm not saying anything of the kind. I'm trying to explain why I lost my head. Pressure had been building up inside me ever since our wedding morning, I suppose. I've been bewildered—not knowing what had gone wrong between us, not able to get any sense out of you. I was angry, frustrated . . .'

'Oh,' she said scathingly. 'You were frustrated, were you? I wasn't behaving like a meek little bride so you decided to teach me a lesson?'

Dark red ran along his cheekbones and his eyes glittered. 'You're deliberately twisting everything I say! That wasn't what I meant. I was under pressure and it suddenly snapped.' He swung away and prowled to the window, his long bare legs loping, the sunlight showing her dark body hair scattered along his back. Staring out into the garden he said tersely, 'I'm only human.'

'What am I, then?' she asked in a cold, pointed voice. 'How do you think I feel? Do you think I enjoyed that display of macho barbarism? Because if that's what's in your mind, forget it. It made me sick.'

She heard the harsh intake of his breath, saw his lean body stiffen, but he didn't try to answer her, although the silence in the room vibrated with his angry emotion, and contrarily she resented the fact that he didn't say anything.

What was the point in talking yet, anyway?

They weren't using the same language. Sean wouldn't understand the confused tangle of motives making her act the way she was and she couldn't tell him how simple it could all be if he really felt anything for her. She had hated it when he used force and violence on that beach, but it wasn't his lovemaking she had been rejecting—it had been the way he had tried to compel her. There was a principle at stake; but Sean was not a man to whom principles mattered. It was winning he cared about—he had tried coaxing and diplomacy and they hadn't worked, so in the last resort he had fallen back on that old male tactic—force.

Part of her bitterness was the knowledge that if he had used a very different strategy he might have won hands-down, in spite of her careful intentions. She was vulnerable to Sean's lovemaking; when he was near her she felt the blood singing in her ears and her body trembling. When he touched her she became blind with desire, she couldn't think, she let go of all her principles and rational intentions, her mind submerged beneath the clamour of her body.

Sean hadn't guessed that, thank heavens. He had tried to storm the citadel whose gates he could so easily have coaxed to open; and ironically made it impossible for himself to win, although she had no intention of letting him know that. She was far too angry with him; the reverberations of her shock still sent tremors through her body, it would be a long time before she got over the fear she had felt or the bitter helplessness of being unable to stop him if he seriously intended to take her. If he had, it would have been destructive for both of them. How could either of them forget it? When she gave herself to him she wanted an exchange of love, a mutual satisfaction, not a battlefield with herself as the loser and Sean playing the age-old masculine role of conqueror.

He suddenly swung round and faced her. 'Shouting at each other won't get us anywhere. We're here for two weeks—if we're going to have all this anger, we're going to have a pretty miserable fortnight. Can't you forget it ever happened? Start again?'

She considered him through her lowered lashes. 'It will never happen again?' she asked warily, and he took a quick stride towards her.

'I give you my word.' He gave her a coaxing smile and she watched him with ironic eyes, seeing the hopeful gleam in those dark eyes and sure she was reading his mind. Sean was afraid he had wrecked his chances by his outburst on the beach and he was trying to re-establish a relationship with her. He had at least realised the magnitude of his error, she thought drily. That was something. He wouldn't try force again, and perhaps in time he might even begin to work out what it was she was holding out for. She almost felt sorry for him for a second; he was like a mole burrowing through darkness and unable to see his destination.

She held on to one tiny thread of hope—Sean's attention was totally fixed on her now, however it had wandered in the past. If he cared anything for her they might still have a future—she wouldn't know until Sean knew himself, but she could be patient. He was worth waiting for.

'Okay, it's a deal,' she said lightly and saw his mouth relax, heard the sigh of relief he gave.

Over the next few days they slid into an enjoyable routine; spending each morning on the beach, swimming and sunbathing, going back into the villa for a light lunch and spending the afternoon driving around the island in the car Sean had hired. They had dinner out in the evenings; there were a number of excellent fish restaurants only a short drive away, they picked a different one each night. Miranda enjoyed the drive back to the villa late at night; leaning back in the seat next to Sean in a companionable silence, watching the stars glitter high in the dark blue sky and the moonlight drift silently on the sea.

One morning she overslept and Sean woke her with a cup of coffee, leaning over to shake her awake. Her eyes opened drowsily and she gazed at him for a second, the strongly featured tanned face only inches away.

'Time to wake up, Sleeping Beauty,' he said softly.

'Right name, wrong one of us,' Miranda murmured, smiling at him as her heart flipped over with pleasure in the very sight of him.

His brows rose. 'What?' He began to laugh and Miranda eyed him wryly, then sat up and reached for her coffee, her nose quivering in appreciation of the delicious fragrance. Sean suddenly stopped laughing, watching her with a frown.

'What did you mean by that crack?' he asked as she sipped the strong black liquid.

She looked at him through her lashes, smiling teasingly. 'Oh, one day your princess will come, maybe.'

He put a hand to her ruffled hair, stroking it back from her sleep-flushed face. 'I don't like it when you talk in riddles. I thought you were such a straightforward girl but I was wrong, wasn't I?'

'About that, too,' she agreed.

'What else was I wrong about?' he asked quickly.

'You're always asking me questions, but you don't seem keen on answering any of mine,' she evaded.

He sat back, his bare shoulders tanned and smooth. He was already in his swimming trunks and looked as if he had been up for hours. They had got back to the villa very late last night and Miranda had been heavy with sleep. She marvelled at the way Sean seemed able to burn the candle at both ends; he got up very early every day and went to bed very late, but then that was, no doubt, a habit picked up in his working life. He had to drive himself hard to keep up with the pressure of his job; top executives rarely get a chance to relax and when they do find it hard to unwind.

'Ask away,' Sean challenged, his muscled body apparently at ease, but she saw that betraying tic beating beside his mouth and knew he wasn't as relaxed as he tried to look.

'Did my father suggest that you marry me?' She delivered her question coolly and saw the tightening of his face, the flick of his lashes as he looked down to consider his answer. She watched him intently; trying to guess whether he would tell her the truth or evade the question again.

He looked up. 'Yes.' His voice was flat and without intonation. 'He started dropping hints long before I met you. I took no notice, he was so obvious about it that I decided you must be as ugly as sin or he wouldn't be worrying about getting you married. It seemed an open and shut case of a man with a very plain daughter and no son to inherit his business and I frankly wasn't interested, he merely embarrassed me. Whenever he started talking about you I tried to change the subject.'

Miranda swallowed on a wave of pain. How could her father have done that to her? Resentment kept her silent and Sean looked at her hard, his eyes uncertain.

'All that was before I met you, though,' he said, and she gave him a bitter smile.

'You weren't interested but you still asked me for a date the first time we met!'

'I'd seen you then!' he protested as though she was being stupid not to realise the difference that made.

'If I had been as ugly as sin would anything have been different?'

He shifted angrily, his brows jerking together. 'I asked you out because I wanted to get to know you, not because your father had suggested it! If we hadn't got on, I wouldn't have asked you out again.'

She gave him a sarcastic smile, her dark blue eyes glowing with cynical disbelief. 'No?'

'No!' he exploded, getting up. 'I shouldn't have told you the truth, should I? You're so fixated on what your father tried to do, that you refuse to see that what I actually did had nothing to do with his plans. I started dating you because I wanted to, not because your father pushed me into it. I'm quite capable of telling him to get lost. I'm damned good at my job and I'm too important to him to need to please him by dating his daughter.'

'It wasn't that simple, though, was it?' She put down her cup and swung her legs out of the bed, her pink cotton nightie floating down to her knees. 'When you control my trust fund you have a big say in what happens in the company and eventually when my father retires . . .'

'He'll never retire,' Sean interrupted brusquely. 'He wouldn't voluntarily give up control of the company, don't you know him better than that?' He walked to the door, his long bare legs moving in angry strides. As his hand grasped the door handle he threw a glowering look at her over his shoulder. 'There's no way I'm going to persuade you that you're wrong about me, is there? I'm crazy to try. I can talk until I'm blue in the face, but you've made up your mind and nothing I can say makes any impression. You're quite prepared to take half the truth and decide that the rest is lies because you've decided that I'm an unscrupulous bastard without any feelings.' He stopped abruptly, his face dark red, then burst out harshly: 'Well, I resent it! If that's how you see me, why did you ever agree to marry me? If you'd ever really loved me you'd know me well enough to realise my pride wouldn't let me get to the top by using a woman. I don't need to stoop to tactics like that—if I did, I'd think less of myself.'

Miranda sat on the edge of the bed, staring at him, shaken by the violence in his voice. She couldn't get a word out and the silence dragged by for a minute.

'I'm going down to swim,' Sean grated when she didn't answer. He slammed the door behind him as he went and she winced at the crash.

She might have believed what he had just said if she hadn't remembered so vividly the lack of conviction in his lovemaking during the months before their marriage. Sean had dated her half-heartedly, his mind always on something else. He hadn't been in love with her, or felt that he had to give her all his attention. He had gone through the successive stages of their relationship like a man performing a ritual in which he has no real belief; their first kiss, their intimate dinners, their gradual acceptance as a publicly acknowledged pair and then their formal engagement and their wedding plans. Looking back on those months she suspected that Sean hadn't woken up to what it all meant. He had decided to marry her and calmly proceeded to do what was necessary. Was he deluding himself when he insisted that he hadn't married her because her father wanted him to? Had he fooled himself as much as her? Perhaps he had had to convince himself that he wanted to marry her for her own sake and not because of the money and power she would bring him, because it would have dented his self-respect to admit that his motives were less than admirable. It was so easy to fool oneself when the stakes were high.

Sighing, she walked into the shower room and turned on the spray of water. When she had showered and dried herself she went back into the bedroom and picked out a vivid yellow bikini and a transparent gauzy yellow beach coat to wear over it.

She felt hungry, so before she went down to the beach she ate some croissants at the table in the dining alcove looking over the garden. The maid had visited the villa twice in the last few days and replenished the food stores as well as cleaning the rooms. She was a large, cheerful woman with four children, some of whom came with her on her visits to the villa. She had told Miranda that she looked after half a dozen holiday villas; she had a thriving business working on contract to a local estate agent. She had offered to keep them supplied with food, which, Miranda suspected, she bought on commission from some local shopkeeper with whom she had a deal, but it was worth the slight extra cost for the convenience of not having to shop oneself.

Far below on the silvery beach Miranda saw

Sean's black head bobbing among the curling waves. She watched him, her eyes wistful. She hated the bitterness and conflict which entered into all their conversations whenever they became personal, but she had no option but to reject him if he tried to come too close. She would despise herself if she allowed their marriage to become a real one while she knew that Sean didn't love her—occasionally she felt flickers of hope, when she met his eyes and saw his smile, immediate and genuine with no ulterior motive behind it. Was she crazy to hope that Sean cared more for her than he knew? Was she deluding herself when she played for time in the hope that their marriage might still have a chance? She couldn't relinquish all hope of that. She loved him too much and she was beginning to see that if Sean had not really been attracted to her, he wouldn't have got so angry when she kept him at arms' length.

That didn't mean that he hadn't married her just because it suited his business plans, of course. But it might mean that the physical attraction she was beginning to be sure he felt, could become something as deep as the feelings she had for him. Sean might have married her at the prompting of his head, but she suspected that he was blind to the urges of his heart.

Getting up with a sigh she cleared the table and dumped the crockery into the sink to wash it up before going down to the beach. She had just finished the washing-up when there was a ring on the front door bell.

Surprised, she wiped her hands, took off the

tiny apron she had worn, and went to answer it.
For a second she stared blankly at the man
outside, not recognising him and baffled by the
large cellophane-wrapped bouquet of flowers he
held out to her. Briefly it flashed across her mind
that Sean had sent them and her heartmissed a
beat, then she suddenly realised that her visitor
was the man she had found half-drowned on the
beach. He smiled ruefully at her.

'Forgotten me already? I'm crushed.'

Miranda laughed. 'No, of course I remember
you—it isn't every day I pull a fish out of the sea
and it turns out to be a man.'

He laughed. 'I brought you a thank you
offering.'

She took the flowers slowly, staring at them.
'Thank you—gracious, what gorgeous flowers,
it's very kind of you.'

'A few flowers for my life? I wish I could do a
lot more.'

'I must put them in water right away,' Miranda
said, backing, and he followed her into the
kitchen and watched as she unwrapped the
flowers and found two vases for them after a long
hunt through the kitchen cupboards. Marty
talked while he watched her. He put a neatly
paper-wrapped parcel on a cabinet top.

'I brought your robe back, thanks for lending it
to me. I've had it laundered. I'd have brought it
back sooner, but I only got it from the hotel
laundry today, they aren't exactly on the ball. I
think most of them are half-asleep all day.
Getting them to do anything is a mammoth task.'

She smiled at him over her shoulder as she clipped the stalks of the flowers. 'Did you ever get your sailboard back?'

'It wasn't mine—it belonged to the hotel sports club,' he said wryly. 'They tell me they're putting the cost on my bill.'

'Tough luck! An expensive day all round, wasn't it?'

'It had its compensations. I met you.'

She looked at him with amusement. 'Aren't you nice?' She slid the flowers into their vases and stood back to admire them. 'They're beautiful, thank you very much.'

'My pleasure,' he said, watching her from the door. She carried both vases into the lounge and Marty followed her, watching her arrange them in the best positions.

Shooting a wary look over his shoulder he asked, 'Is your husband out? Or still in bed? I hope my arrival didn't disturb him.'

It would have done if Sean had been around, but Miranda gave no hint of that as she smiled at him, walking out of the lounge and hovering in the hall.

'He's down on the beach, swimming.'

She saw Marty's slim figure relax and his eyes brighten.

'I can't say I'm sorry to hear that,' he admitted frankly with a grin. 'He didn't take to me, did he?' His eyes wandered down her slim, curved body in the delicate gauzy coat through which her bikini showed clearly. 'And I can't blame him with a wife like you.'

Miranda was amused by his cheerful admiration. 'Want some coffee?' she offered, moving back from the door.

He was through it like a shot. 'I thought you'd never ask.'

'I'll have to make a fresh pot—I've just drunk most of this and anyway it's lukewarm by now.' She spooned coffee into the percolator and Marty strolled over to the dining alcove to stare out of the window.

'Your husband swims well, he looks athletic—I can almost see the muscles in his arms from here. I wouldn't like to get on the wrong side of him.'

Miranda turned to glance at him as she took down two clean cups from the kitchen cabinet. He looked very fit himself; his slim body tanned and lean in the white running vest and very brief white shorts. His hair was sun-bleached above the dark bronze of his face, but he did not have Sean's magnetic sexuality, he was far too laid back and casual. Marty had a hedonistic air; she had a feeling he was a drifter, which, no doubt, explained why he lived abroad in an alien society. He wouldn't need to put down roots, or feel he belonged wherever he worked. He merely lived from day to day.

'Have you got any family in England?' she asked and he nodded.

'Oh, sure. I'll be seeing them when I go there next week—a few days of them is enough for me, though. While I'm back home I'll look up a few old friends, maybe take a trip to Scotland to do some fishing.'

'You like sport?' The coffee had begun to bubble and Miranda turned to watch it, hearing him moving back towards her.

'I've always enjoyed being active.' Marty reached out a hand suddenly and picked up the floating edge of her beach coat. 'This is pretty—very sexy, too, especially with that bikini under it.'

She looked up at him drily. 'Don't flirt, Marty, I'm married, remember.'

He was very close, his eyes lazy, his smile rueful. 'Pity,' he said and she couldn't help laughing at his expression.

'I'm flattered, but . . .'

'Can't I tempt you?' he asked mock-mournfully, but there was good-humoured acceptance in his smile. Before Miranda could answer him they both heard the footstep on the parquet floor and Marty sprang back from her as if shot in the back, his smile vanishing as he looked round.

Sean wasn't smiling, either. He stared insistently at Miranda, his jawline rigid. 'Well?' he demanded in a harsh voice. 'Answer the man. Can he tempt you?'

CHAPTER SEVEN

MIRANDA stayed calm, turning to switch off the percolator. 'You're just in time for coffee,' she said with her back to Sean, getting out another cup.

'It was just a joke,' Marty offered in the voice of a man wishing the floor would open up and swallow him.

'I'm not laughing,' Sean assured him.

Miranda turned, smiling sweetly. 'My husband loves stating the obvious.' She picked up the coffee pot. 'Do you take cream and sugar, Marty?'

He looked at his watch and smote his brow. 'My God, look at the time—I've got an appointment at eleven—I'm never going to make it. Sorry, I'd have loved to have some coffee but another time.' He caught Sean's cold gaze and backed away. 'Well, thanks again for the loan of the robe and for saving my life,' he mumbled to Miranda. 'I'll be off.'

Sean moved to hold the door open, looking as if he would love to speed their unwanted guest on his way. Marty vanished and Sean slammed the door after him. Miranda was pouring herself some more coffee; she didn't really want it but she was so angry she was acting automatically.

Sean came into the kitchen again and leaned on the doorframe in a pointed way. 'How long has he been here?'

She shrugged. 'Ten minutes.'

His eye roved up and down her; coolly assessing the brief bikini and the drifting transparent beach coat which showed every curve of her body. She saw his mouth twist and her eyes flashed resentfully. How dare he look at her like that, as though he had caught her in some compromising situation?

'Long enough,' he drawled and she spat back at him.

'For what?'

'Oh, come on, I don't have to spell it out.' He was sarcastic now, his smile chilly.

'Oh, yes, you do, if you can't put what you're insinuating into plain English accusation, don't bother to hint.' Her face was flushed with temper and her teeth met as he gave her another of those tight smiles.

'I'm not suggesting you took him to bed . . .'

'Well, thanks!' she interrupted fiercely.

He carried on, ignoring her. 'But that guy was here to make a pass at you and we both know it. It was obvious he fancied you the day you brought him up here, I knew he'd be back.'

'He brought back your robe, which he had had laundered—his manners are good, even if yours are atrocious.'

'I don't make passes at other men's wives.'

'You don't even make them at your own,' she threw back before she could stop herself and then stood, mouth open and eyes aghast, while Sean watched her with lifting brows and a slow relaxation of his hard mouth.

'Well, well,' he murmured, amusement glinting

in his eyes. 'Why didn't you tell me before?'

With alarm she saw him moving towards her and backed, her breathing impeded. 'That wasn't an invitation,' she said sharply, putting a hand out to hold him away.

He took it firmly and pulled, smiling in a way she found maddening. Digging her heels in like a recalcitrant mule she refused to come any closer, shaking her head, and Sean took another step, putting her arm around his waist and holding it there.

'Stop it,' Miranda said breathlessly, because this was not going the way she had intended. She had never seen Sean in this mood; it threw her, she didn't know how to cope with him. There was something glimmering in his dark eyes that made her pulses beat far too fast.

'We had a bargain, remember?' she said, almost with desperation, as he put a hand to her cheek and stroked light fingers down the flushed skin.

'You change your mind so often,' he said, a finger drifting along her unsteady mouth, staring down at it as he touched it. He was almost close against her now, his body an inch away so that she felt the warmth of his skin. 'First you don't want me to make a pass at you, then you complain because I haven't—is this an example of female unpredictability?' His fingers were sliding down her throat now, she felt the cool trickle of their descent as if drops of water ran over her skin, and shivered.

'I didn't mean . . . what you thought I meant,' she stammered in confusion.

His eyes mocked her. 'Didn't you, Miranda?'
He bent and brushed his mouth along her cheek
and the exploring hand closed over one of her
breasts, sending a shiver of wild response
through her. Instinctively her hand clutched at
his back and he let go of her wrist, his hand now
free to move gently along the curve of her hip.

'Don't,' Miranda said vaguely; her eyes closing
and her lips yielding to the caress of his mouth.

'Don't you like it?' Sean asked, laughing
softly, his kiss deepening and his arm going
round her waist to pull her closer. She scarcely
heard the teasing question, her senses were going
crazy, she was touching his smooth bare back
with hands that shook. Heat burned through her
and as Sean lifted his head to look at her, she let
her face fall against his shoulder, hiding that
betraying flush. His skin smelled of the sea;
helplessly she touched her lips to it and trembled,
her kiss sliding along the muscled line of warm
flesh, rough with salt bloom which she tasted
with the tip of her tongue.

Sean gave a faint smothered gasp. He was
stroking her hair with one hand while the other
gently moulded her body, discovering the shape
and contour without haste.

She felt him unhook her bikini top and a fierce
shudder of pleasure shot through her as his
fingers closed over her breasts. She lifted her
head blindly, searching for his mouth, past any
pretence and too weak with desire to care. They
kissed, their bodies clinging, skin to skin, the full
warmth of her breasts against the lean power of

his chest, thighs brushing, her hands moving convulsively up and down his back, and when she felt him unhook her bikini panties she made no protest. Naked under the filmy beach coat she moved even closer, her fingers clenched in his black hair, holding his head down while she kissed him hungrily.

Sean's hands clasped her waist and lifted her, without his mouth moving from her lips, and he began to walk slowly, carrying her, locked in that kiss, so that she felt as if she was floating, weightless and helpless to stop what was happening. The quiet little voice of her intelligence sharply denied that, but Miranda chose to ignore her mind, she had listened to it long enough. She wanted Sean with a feverish desire that seemed like necessity. If she stopped him now, she would die of frustration.

Sean put her down in the bedroom and his head lifted, breaking off their long kiss. She wouldn't open her eyes, she was afraid to break the hectic spell of his lovemaking, she stood, shuddering, as he bent and kissed her breasts, a hand cupping each, his tongue warm and tantalising as it flickered over her nipples. His mouth moved down the centre of her body, exploring her navel softly, before moving on over the flat plane of her belly. Miranda breathed harshly as Sean knelt to bury his face between her thighs, his palms clasping her smooth-skinned legs.

They had never made love like this before. Sean's lovemaking had been careful and always he had broken off before it became intimate. She had wondered at times if he would ever touch her the way she needed to be touched, show her the passion she longed to have from him. She had even suspected he was cold, but she had no such doubts now. The intimate invasion of his mouth drove her wild, and she held his head, running her fingers through his thick hair, the strands clinging to her perspiring skin.

He stood up unsteadily and she looked at him through her lashes. He was darkly flushed and breathing raggedly, his features so taut that he looked unfamiliar, dangerous. Silently, he pushed her backwards on to the bed, and her limp body obeyed, tumbling down as if her muscles no longer existed.

Sean came down on her a moment later. Naked now, the force of his body pushed her down into the mattress and she gave a breathless gasp, her eyes opening fully, the dark blue iris languid and glazed with passion.

'You're heavy!' she protested shakily.

He gave her a crooked little smile, the muscled brown line of his throat stretched in tension as he arched over her. 'Am I? I'm sorry, I was in too much of a hurry to remember . . . but that's your fault, isn't it? You've kept me waiting so long my patience has run out.' He bent his head and buried his mouth in the deep, shadowy cleft between her breasts, groaning. 'I want you now, quickly, no more games, Miranda.' His teeth grazed softly over her nipples. 'You've been tormenting me ever since we got here. Do you

think it was easy to sleep in the same room with you every night and keep my hands to myself? Why do you think I went to bed so late and got up so early? If I hadn't this would have happened the first night.'

Miranda lay still, listening with a frown. The urgency of his body told her how much he wanted her, now, at this moment—but if she let him take her, what would it resolve? Her own frustration and need of him, yes, that, but if Sean won so easy a victory their marriage would soon fall apart. She had held his attention by keeping him at arms' length—once he had sated the male desire for possession, wouldn't his interest lapse?

She should never have let him go this far, she should never have given in to the cravings of her own desire for him. How was she going to get out of this room?

She thought rapidly, her eyes agitated, then pushed one hand into the ruffled coils of his black hair, pulling at it. 'Sean . . .'

'Ssh,' he groaned, reluctantly lifting his head. 'No more talking, Miranda, not now. We've got better things to do and you've tantalised me long enough.'

'Just answer one question first!'

He sighed, closing his eyes, then opening them to look at her drily. 'I don't like the sound of that—you've already asked too many questions and you're never satisfied with the answers.'

'Were you in love with me when you asked me to marry you?' she asked before he could start making love to her again, and she watched him

intently as she asked. He looked startled, taken
aback, then he began to frown, his eyes full of an
angry confusion.

'Why do women always ask damn fool
questions like that?' he grated, sliding off her
and sitting up, the muscles in his back clenched.
'What do you want me to do? Lie to you? Feed
you a fairy tale to make it easy for you to do
what you know damned well you want to do,
anyway? I wasn't sure until now that you did
want me, but now I am, Miranda. You may not
want to admit it, but I could make you in five
minutes—I just did, in case you hadn't noticed.'
His voice altered, the timbre of it becoming
deep and husky, sending shivers down her
spine. He looked round at her and smiled
unsteadily. 'It's so simple, don't you see that? I
want you and you want me, and we're married,
which makes it easy enough to admit how we
feel, I'd have thought.'

She felt a bitter aching in her throat but she
managed a faint smile. 'You aren't talking about
_eelings, though, Sean—you're talking about
something far more basic. What you're saying is
that I could be any woman—if I was attractive
enough you'd enjoy making love to me, and
maybe you'd walk away afterwards and forget my
very name.'

Impatiently he snapped, 'Why drag in hypothetical questions? You're not just any woman.
You're my wife and I won't be walking away
afterwards, we're going to build a life together
and the sooner we start the better.' He turned

back towards her and she held him off with one hand, her face pale.

'Put the hypothetical question another way, Sean—what if I would be just as happy sleeping with Marty Knox?'

His eyes hardened. 'And would you?'

'You're missing the point—if it doesn't matter whether you're in love or not and sex is just a matter of physical need why should I prefer you to him?'

He was very still, staring at her intently, his jawline rigid. 'You're a little late to think about that. We are married, and if you're wondering if you wouldn't be happier with him, I'm sorry, you're not getting the option.'

'Marriages don't have to be final,' she said wearily. She wasn't getting anywhere; he refused to understand, perhaps he was incapable of loving.

'This one is,' Sean said with a terse determination which made her shiver. He stared down at her, obstinacy in every line of him. 'Miranda, I could lie to you easily enough, but I won't do that because what sort of life would we have together if I couldn't be honest with you about the very centre of our marriage? I'm not the romantic type of guy. I'm not even sure I know what they mean by being "in love". I've never been "in love" with anyone. I've always been too busy to waste my time mooning over a girl. Sex— that I understand. That's a biological urge we all feel. Affection, that I understand, too. I'm very fond of you, I like you a lot although you puzzle me at times. I enjoy being with you, I'd miss you if you weren't around, and you matter more to me than any other woman I've ever met. If any of that adds up to what you mean by being in love then maybe we're just arguing over semantics.'

She laughed bitterly. 'No, Sean—we aren't talking about the same thing. Diana was right . . .'

His eyes narrowed, bright and alert. 'Diana? Diana who?'

She hadn't realised what she was saying and flushed in confused wariness, looking away. 'Oh, it doesn't matter.'

'It does if the lady has been giving opinions on me and my marriage,' Sean said flatly. 'I only know one Diana—how many do you know? Or are we both talking about your father's secretary?'

She shrugged. 'Okay, that's who I meant.' What did it matter anyway? There was no reason why he shouldn't know, now.

'What was she right about?' he asked and she hesitated.

'Oh, she said you'd married me for . . .'

'Your father's company?' he finished for her when she paused again. 'So that's where you got the idea from! Well, I see I shall have to show Miss Cobbold my gratitude for ruining my honeymoon. What else did she tell you?'

'She didn't actually tell me anything—I overheard her talking to someone.' Miranda was flushed and unhappy about this discussion; it made her nauseous to remember the other woman's malicious amusement and the vile comments she had made about Sean and Ferdy.

'She was discussing my private affairs with someone else? My God, is this gossip all round the firm?' Dark red had invaded Sean's face and his mouth was a hard line.

'She was talking to her cousin. I doubt if she's mentioned it to anyone else.'

'Her cousin? The guy who works in sales?'

Miranda laughed angrily. 'You know more than I do.'

He ran a hand through his black hair, smoothing it down in an impatient gesture. 'When was this?'

'At my party,' she whispered.

'The night before our wedding?' He didn't wait for her to nod, he swore softly. 'I see—and you believed every word? That's why you bolted and tried to stop the wedding?' There was a long pause then he swung off the bed and began to get dressed rapidly. She pulled a sheet over her, her skin icy.

When he was wearing a pair of shorts and a dark blue cotton T-shirt, Sean walked back to the bed and stood there, his hands on his hips and his legs apart in an aggressive stance.

'Right, tell me everything you overheard. Don't leave anything out—I want to know the precise state of the damage.' A short time ago he had been an impatient lover, now he was a curt businessman demanding explanations from an unwilling witness. Miranda didn't think she liked him much in either persona—for he was neither human nor vulnerable, and for love to exist there must be a degree of vulnerability.

'I don't like Diana,' Miranda said. 'In fact, I loathe her, but what she was saying happened to be the truth. I suppose I knew it all along, but it wasn't until I heard her saying it aloud that I accepted the fact. She didn't know I was listening, she didn't intend me to hear. You can't do much about a private conversation.'

'I can make sure Ferdy knows all about it,' Sean said grimly. 'She's his confidential secretary—if she gossips about his private life, what else does she tell her cousin and God knows who else?'

'Oh, I doubt if she talks to anyone else the way she did to him,' Miranda said with irony. She looked quickly at Sean, hesitated, then said, 'She plans to marry my father, did you know that?'

His face was impassive. 'Is that something else you overheard?'

'Yes, she talked about it quite openly.' Miranda suddenly remembered something and gave a derisive smile. 'She said that if she had a son your plans would be ruined.'

His mouth twisted. 'Charming lady.'

'It would spike your guns, though, wouldn't it?' she mocked and he gave her a level stare.

'You seem quite pleased by the prospect.'

'It would have a certain irony, wouldn't it? After all you've done to get the company . . . I don't think Diana believes in love, either. She can't or she wouldn't be planning anything so coldblooded, but perhaps watching you at work put the idea into her head?'

'You flatter me,' he said with biting sarcasm.

'Do you think so?' Her brows lifted and he eyed her thoughtfully.

'You're full of surprises, Miranda—you've shown me more sides to your character in the last few days than you ever did before we were married. You have a tongue like a scorpion when you choose.' He moved to the door and looked back at her huddled figure on the bed, his eyes wry. 'You've asked me why I married you and I've been frank—isn't it time you told me why you married me?'

She hadn't expected that and he took her by surprise. Her lips parted on a faint gasp and she bit her inner lip to keep it steady, wondering how on earth to answer him. The last thing she could do was tell him the truth—after his admission that he wasn't in love with her, she would die rather than let him know how she felt about him.

She fell back on evasion. 'I'm beginning to wonder that, myself.'

Sean waited, watching her. 'Is that all the answer I'm going to get?'

'For the moment,' Miranda said lightly, and she shrugged.

'I'm going for a drive—do you want to come? Or are you going down to swim?'

'I'll come. It won't take me a minute to dress.'

When he had gone she sat there for a moment, staring at nothing, her face set in lines of melancholy. She had known, of course. Sean had never been in love with her, he had at least admitted that now. It was some tiny shred of comfort that he had also said he had never been in love with anyone else, but Miranda couldn't find much comfort even in that. She felt like crying, but she wouldn't give in to such weakness now.

She forced herself off the bed and hurriedly dressed. The days here seemed to drag past— they should have been the happiest of her life. Instead they were among the most miserable she had ever spent. If anyone ever mentioned the word honeymoon to her again she would scream.

Oddly, though, their row seemed to have cleared the air between them. Sean drove right across the island through winding, badly made roads on which they jolted so violently that Miranda got the giggles and Sean started laughing too when on one occasion she shot up in her seat and seemed about to be ejected from the car.

Gasping, she yelled at him, 'It isn't funny— slow down!'

'You looked like a surprised jack-in-the-box,' he teased.

'This car hasn't got any springs!'

'It hasn't got much petrol, either—you'd better pray we don't run out before we hit the coast or you have a long walk in front of you.'

She gave him a wicked look. 'If any other man told me that, I'd be suspicious.'

His mouth twitched in amusement. 'I've never had to use such corny old tricks.'

'I see, the girls just flocked, did they?' she mocked, wondering at the same time how many others there had been before her. Sean had never been communicative about his past life.

His face sobered slightly. 'I told you, I've never given much attention to a private life. Oh, there were girls, but I hadn't enough energy to spare for any of them to be important to me.'

'Only your career mattered?' Miranda watched him, frowning. Was ambition the only driving force in his life? Had it driven out every other interest?

'I had Declan to take care of and very little money to spare. My parents didn't leave much. I had to be successful.' He drove on in silence for a few moments then said abruptly: 'And it was part of my nature, I suppose. I don't know why I'm made that way—do any of us understand ourselves? I suppose a psychologist would say that being the eldest child made me feel responsible for Declan and determined to get on, or maybe I can blame heredity.' He grimaced wryly. 'I've never seen any point in trying to work out what made me tick. That's how I am and understanding why makes very little difference.'

'To you, maybe—but it might to other people,' she said gently, and he gave her a quick, searching look.

'To you, you mean?'

'Perhaps,' she evaded.

He stared ahead, looking oddly puzzled, even taken aback. Miranda studied his sharp-edged profile with a half-bitter tenderness. She began to think that Sean was emotionally undeveloped, unused to sharing or the give and take of love. Had the death of his parents anything to do with that? She sighed. Perhaps he was right—knowing why made no real difference, one had to cope with how things were, and Sean was apparently unable to surrender himself to emotion except in a limited range. He felt strongly enough when it came to possession; his reaction to Marty had showed her that. Sean could be jealous, he could feel desire, be determined to take and hold on to what he had acquired. It was in the gentler, warmer field of emotion that he was empty. For her the essential question was: could he change? Would he ever learn to care for her in any other way than as a woman he wanted to possess?

They just made it to a garage before the petrol ran out, and drove on with a full tank to a small restaurant beside a busy harbour where they had lunch; eating sea food in leisurely enjoyment under the shade of a red and yellow striped blind while they watched fishermen mending nets and the bustle and noise of the little town. It was the best day they had spent together on the island, and when they set off back to the villa much later in the day Miranda was drowsy with sun and sea air. She fell asleep with her head on Sean's shoulder, only waking when he parked outside the villa.

It wasn't until they walked into the lounge that the harmony between them changed. Sean halted abruptly in front of a table, staring at the vase of flowers on it. 'Where did these come from? Are they from the garden?'

Miranda fixed a neutral expression on her face. 'No, Marty brought them.'

He turned and stared at her, his eyes like gimlets, but he seemed to have nothing to say. She would have given a great deal to know what he was thinking.

CHAPTER EIGHT

THEY flew back into London in the middle of a snowstorm. Miranda peered out of the plane window at whirling white flakes, her face incredulous. The pilot had cheerfully informed them that the weather in the U.K. was bad, but she hadn't actually expected a blizzard to be raging in the middle of April, even in England. Snow ploughs were out on some back roads as they drove from Heathrow, and traffic was appalling. It was moving, but as slowly as flies caught in glycerine, and drivers' tempers were short. Horns blared all round them as Sean edged his way along the road.

Miranda huddled in her thin coat, shivering. The windscreen wipers clacked uselessly and snow built up on the glass so that Sean had to peer closely to see where he was going. Their new home was not yet quite ready; it was being totally redecorated and although it should have been completed before their wedding the contractor had not kept his promise. He blamed his suppliers, but Sean had grimly told the man that he would take legal action if the decorating was not finished by the end of April. In the meantime they were going to spend a week with Ferdy since Sean had already sold his London flat. Their new house had been Ferdy's wedding present to Miranda, although it was legally a joint possession.

Sean turned his head to look at her as he halted at some traffic lights. 'Won't be long now—cold?'

'My teeth are chattering,' she agreed and he picked up one of her hands and rubbed it gently, until the blood flowed back into it and the blue tinge left her flesh. While he was intent on that she glanced up at the traffic lights and saw that they had turned amber. 'We're moving again,' she warned and Sean turned his attention back to the road, dropping her hand. The car they were driving had been left at Heathrow that morning since they hadn't been certain which plane they would catch. Ferdy had taken care of transport for them with his usual thoroughness.

Her eyes softened as she stared out of the window at the snowy fields. She couldn't be angry with her father. However much she resented his manipulation of her personal life she knew he had acted with the best of intentions and his caring was touching, it was yet another sign of his love for her, which showed itself in a hundred ways from checking that there would be a car waiting at the airport when she got back to making sure that she had anything else she might need. No detail was too small, Ferdy watched over her like a hen with just one chick. In her teens she might have rebelled against that, but she had lost her mother at a time which made her intensely aware of her own need for affection, and by the same token aware of her father's need for it. Circumstance had made her sensitive to a human need for love and the expression of it.

She watched Sean's calm profile wistfully. He had never discovered what she had learnt at an early age, but it wasn't too late to cure his emotional myopia. Sometimes, over the past week, she had begun to hope that he had changed in some indefinable way. They had spent most of the second part of their visit lazing around on the beach; swimming and sunbathing, eating salad and fruit, reading in contented silence together or discussing odd subjects which came up out of nowhere, from what they read in a newspaper or remembered from childhood, from current affairs or the theatre. It had been the sort of free floating exchange of views and attitudes that they had never indulged in before their marriage; there had never been time, Sean had never been in a casually relaxed mood before.

It seemed extraordinary to her at times, but she knew that she had got to know him better over the past two weeks than she ever had before. He had surprised, even disturbed her, but at the same time he had amused and often delighted her. She hadn't had time to sort out her impressions; they were confused and chaotic as yet. No doubt over the coming weeks she would sift through them all and understand even more than she did now what sort of man she had married in such a haphazard, unaware fashion. Had Sean had the same surprises? Was he silently assessing all that he had learnt about her?

Considering his absorbed profile, she smiled wryly. They had married as strangers, but although their relationship was still technically platonic she felt a new intimacy with him, their two weeks alone had formed a tentative pair bonding that the six months preceding it had not achieved.

Peering through the windscreen as he braked suddenly, Sean muttered, 'This weather is unbelievable. It's taken us twice as long to get here as it normally would, but I dare not take my foot off the brake. We're slipping about all over the road as it is.'

'There's no hurry,' she soothed.

'You're cold, I want to get you home as soon as possible,' he said abstractedly, driving onwards as the car in front moved off again.

Miranda sighed a moment later. 'We'll be back at work on Monday. Let's hope the weather has improved by then.'

'You don't have to work if you don't enjoy it,' he said at once. 'We don't need the money, after all.'

'I do enjoy it,' she contradicted hurriedly. 'I just meant that I'm sorry our holiday is over.' Her admission was husky, uncertain—she wondered if she was wise in telling him that.

He smiled drily without taking his eyes off the snow-besieged road ahead. 'It wasn't a holiday— it was a *honeymoon*, contrary to all appearances.'

They were definitely on thin ice with that remark so Miranda looked at her watch and said: 'We should find my father at home when we arrive; it will be well after six by then.' Sean murmured agreement, accepting the change of subject.

Night was thickening the colour of the sky, the dull grey becoming a pall of swirling smoke. Sean had switched on his headlights and in their beam the snow seemed to writhe and dance, the flakes dividing and joining as they blew across the road. Miranda was beginning to recognise landmarks and with each one she felt their two weeks alone together receding; soon they would be engulfed in the family and then work would claim Sean, if not herself. The everyday world would drive a wedge between them; Sean would have other things on his mind again. She looked down at her linked hands. The two rings on her left hand glinted up at her, the square-cut sapphire almost the same colour as her eyes, the wedding ring still feeling heavy to her. Time was like this snow storm; it whirled past your blinded eyes, obliterating landmarks and changing everything you knew. The past two weeks had been like a step outside time, now they had to step back into it and she had a nervous fear that she hadn't yet learnt enough about Sean to make their marriage work once they were home.

With a sigh of relief, Sean turned the car into the drive of her home and Miranda saw the lighted windows shining through the darkness, their yellow gleam thrown across the snowy garden. As Sean pulled up outside, the front door opened and Ferdy was there, bearlike in a thick brown sweater, his grey head silver in the light from the snow as he came forward.

'What a day to come home,' he said, hugging her as she ran into his arms. 'Come inside out of

this winter wind. You've got a tan, was your
weather good? Sometimes it can be pretty cold
over there in the spring.' He drew her into the
hall under a light and looked at her, smiling
broadly. 'You look as if you've had a good
holiday.'

'We had marvellous weather, not too hot but
quite sunny enough for me,' she said, smiling at
their housekeeper as she hurried past to help
Sean with the cases. 'Hallo, Mrs Hammond.'

Sean carried the first two cases into the house
and dumped them in the hall with a groan. 'God
knows what you've got in there,' he said to
Miranda. 'She bought enough presents to stock a
shop,' he told Ferdy who laughed and clapped
him warmly on the shoulder.

'Good to see you back, both of you. We've
missed you, haven't we, Mrs Hammond?'

The housekeeper deposited the cases she had
carried in, nodding cheerfully. 'Quiet as a grave,
this house has been without you, Miss Miranda.
We haven't had many visitors.' She looked at
Ferdy. 'Shall I serve the drinks, sir?'

'Do you two want a drink now or would you
rather go up and change first? I thought we'd
have dinner at home tonight. I didn't think you
would want to go out again in this weather.'

Miranda unbuttoned her coat and Mrs
Hammond collected it over her arm while Sean
was closing the front door.

Turning, he said to Ferdy, 'You're quite right,
I wouldn't go out there again for a fortune. We
had a nightmare drive to get here. It's like pea

soup out there and it's getting worse. I could do
with a stiff whisky but first we'll just dash upstairs
for a few minutes. We seem to have been travelling
for days and I want to wash and get out of this shirt.'

He took off his own coat and Mrs Hammond
took that too, smiling at him. 'Your bedroom
should be nice and warm—I've put you in the big
front room on the other side of the corridor from
Mr Boston.' Her smile moved on to Miranda.
'I've switched all your own things in there, Miss
. . . Mrs Hinton. I must get used to calling you
that, mustn't I?'

'You certainly must,' Sean agreed cheerfully,
unaware that Miranda had stiffened. With her
father watching she had to suppress her reaction
to the news that Mrs Hammond had put them in
the large room on the front of the house. It
hadn't even entered her head to think about the
sleeping arrangements until now. As she walked
up the stairs in front of Sean she bit her lower lip
anxiously, wondering what on earth to do. What
possible reason could she give for asking for
another room? Yet how could she possibly share
that particular room with Sean?

The minute he walked into the room he halted,
staring at the double bed. Miranda felt his eyes
flash sideways to her averted face and picked up
the sudden amusement inside him.

'Now there's a problem,' he said mockingly.
'What *are* you going to do, Miranda?'

'At this moment, wash and change my dress, I
suppose,' she said without meeting his eyes and
he laughed.

'Okay, keep your cool, but you aren't fooling me. You're wondering how to get out of sharing that bed with me, aren't you? Well, if you're thinking of asking me to be a little gentleman and sleep in an armchair tonight, you can think again. In weather like this I prefer a nice, warm bed.' He paused and added tauntingly, 'Especially with a woman in it.'

'Not this woman!' Miranda threw back.

'Okay, Mrs Houdini, the next move is up to you.' He had unbuttoned his shirt and was sliding out of it, the muscles in his shoulders and arms rippling smoothly.

She grabbed some clean clothes from the wardrobe and headed for the adjoining bathroom without answering him. In the mirror over the vanity unit she stared irritably at her own reflection; her eyes were fever bright and her cheeks much too flushed.

'Well, what are you going to do?' she asked her mirror image but it offered no suggestions. Crazy ideas of claiming to have some contagious disease or waiting until everyone had gone to bed before sneaking downstairs to sit up all night in an armchair flitted through her head, but she dismissed either idea as impracticable. Mrs Hammond would know immediately if she slipped into any other bedroom or slept downstairs in a chair or on a sofa; Miranda knew from her childhood that the housekeeper had eagle eyes and a mind like a trained detective. It wouldn't surprise Miranda if Mrs Hammond could actually read minds or see through walls.

She had always seemed to know precisely what Miranda had been up to, however furtively Miranda had gone about it. That was the trouble with being part of a closely-knit household. Everyone knew what everybody else was doing and thinking. There were no secrets, very little privacy and no escape.

When she came out of the bathroom she found Sean fully dressed again in a black ribbed jersey which clung to his deep chest, and a pair of pale grey cord pants. He had shaved and brushed his black hair. He turned to look at her quizzically.

'Had any bright ideas yet?'

She chose to ignore that, pointedly, walking to the door. 'Ready to go down for that drink now?'

'I've been ready for five minutes,' he complained, following her. 'What were you doing in there—knitting that sweater?' He ran appreciative eyes over her soft pink cashmere top and the smoothly fitting cream wool pants she wore with it. 'Very cuddly,' he approved. 'What every man wants to find in his Christmas stocking.'

'Thank-you so much,' she said in dulcet tones. She liked the compliment but was disturbed by the gleam in his eyes as he offered it. Sean was suddenly in a very mischievous mood and she did not like it, it boded ill for the rest of the evening. Unwittingly, Mrs Hammond had pushed her into a corner and from Sean's wicked expression Miranda felt sure he did not intend to let her escape. He was playing with her like a cat with a trapped mouse and she would have given anything to wipe that smile off his face. As sh went down the stairs she glanced secretly at her watch. It was nearly seven-thirty. She had a few hours in which to come up with an escape route.

Sean came up close to her as she put out a hand to the drawing-room door and she looked up, startled, feeling his arm snake round her waist.

The next second he had flung the door open and entered the room, taking her with him in a casually loving embrace. She just had time to drag a smile into her face before Ferdy looked round, beaming at the sight of them.

'There you both are! We were beginning to suspect you weren't coming down again.' He grinned teasingly at them. 'Come to the fire, you must be frozen. Now what can I get the two of you to drink? Diana and I are way ahead of you, you have several drinks to catch up on. Whisky for you, Sean?'

'Yes, that's just what I need,' Sean said, his eyes narrowing on Diana as she smiled at them from the depth of a brocade armchair by the fire. 'Hallo, Diana, how are you?'

'Fine,' she drawled, stretching the feline curve of her body in the chair with a contented sigh. 'How are the two of you? Was the honeymoon ecstatic?' She purred the question, smiling, but although Ferdy might not hear the undertone of mockery Miranda could and so, she knew from Sean's cool profile, did he, but if he disliked the implications of Diana's question and the barely concealed malice in her catlike eyes, he gave no outward sign of it.

'Never a dull moment,' he returned lightly,

picking up Miranda's hand and lifting it to hi
lips with a sideways smile at her.

'How sweet,' Diana said with another of he
phoney smiles. 'Matrimony suits you, Sean; you
look like a cat who's swallowed the cream.'

Miranda settled on the brocade sofa with Sea
close beside her, his arm resting lightly along he
shoulders in what she knew to be a deliberatel
possessive embrace. Her father had not needed to
ask her what she would drink. When he brough
Sean's whisky he handed her a sweet sherry, th
firelight giving the tawny liquid a rich glow
Ferdy sat down on the opposite side of the fir
from Diana and lifted his own glass toward
them.

'Would a toast be too formal? A long and
happy life together, you two.'

Diana lifted her own glass and went throug
the motions of toasting them, but her smile wa
as false as her eyelashes and Miranda watched he
with hostility. Why had Ferdy invited her her
tonight? It should have been a family occasion
just the three of them for this first night home
Why had he chosen to invite Diana, of all people
to make up a foursome? A shiver ran dow
Miranda's back as she watched the other woma
settle back in her chair, her shapely legs crossed
Was Diana's presence here tonight an ominou
sign? Was Ferdy leading up to some sort o
announcement? Diana looked far too much a
home, her sleek body impossibly spectacular i
what on anyone else might have been describe
as a little black dress, but which on Diana becam

an explosively sexy invitation. The black jersey wool clung, outlining Diana's body from her high pointed breasts to her smoothly rounded hips.

Miranda stared into the fire, feeling cold in spite of its flickering heat. If her father did marry Diana she knew that things would never be the same again for her. Diana would exclude her from this house, somehow, and Ferdy might never even realise what was happening.

'How was the villa?' Ferdy asked and Sean began to describe it and talked about the island scenery and the fabulous fish restaurants they had found.

'I thought something was said about presents,' Ferdy hinted broadly a little while later and Miranda gave a little start as she felt their eyes on her.

'I haven't unpacked them yet,' she said, finishing her sherry and putting down the glass on the low coffee table beside the sofa.

Ferdy's lower lip stuck out in a pretence of a pout. 'Have I got to wait until tomorrow? I want to know what you bought me.'

She laughed, getting up. 'Oh, very well—I'll go and find them,' she said indulgently. 'Anyone would think you were a child.'

Ferdy got up too. 'I'll come and talk to you while you hunt for them,' he said and she knew then that the presents were just an excuse—her father wanted to talk to her alone. Her heart sank. Was he about to tell her that he had decided to marry Diana? How was she going to keep a smile on her face if he did? She knew she couldn't

pretend to like Diana, or be delighted at the ide
of the other woman becoming one of the family
but, on the other hand, how could she bear t
hurt her father if his heart was set on th
marriage?

Ferdy was going to be lonely now and he was
man to whom a family warmth was essential. H
liked women's company, not merely in a sexua
sense, but because he enjoyed all the othe
aspects of femininity. He worked hard for lon
hours; when he came home he liked to relax in
comfortable, soothing atmosphere, with a woma
fussing over him. It wasn't merely that, though—
Ferdy needed to give as well as take, he was
man with a lot of affection to offer.

Miranda felt wearily sad as she went up th
stairs with him. Diana wouldn't either give o
take the affection Ferdy needed; she was acquisitiv
and ambitious but she was not a loving woman.

As he followed her into her bedroom Ferd
asked; 'Now that Sean isn't listening, aren't yo
going to tell me if everything's okay?' His voic
teased but his eyes were concerned and she gav
him a quick answering smile.

'Don't I look happy?' she said lightly.

'There's something,' Ferdy said, staring into he
eyes with probing attention. 'A shadow I don'
like to see. I've been worried ever since you
wedding—you did really want to marry him
didn't you, Miranda? You do love him?'

She had flushed but she did not try to loo
away. 'Yes, I just had a touch of bridal panic for
while.'

Ferdy relaxed slightly, but didn't stop watching her. 'Nothing's wrong, then? I'm imagining things?'

She hesitated, then said: 'It's been a long day, travelling is very tiring—maybe that's why I seem dull.' She unlocked her case and searched for the packages she had placed among the clothes. They had been gift-wrapped at the shops where she bought them. She turned and handed two to Ferdy with a smile. 'I hope you like them.'

He grinned. 'They were just an excuse to snatch a minute alone with you, darling.' He tucked them under his arm. 'I'll open them downstairs.'

She waited, her nerves stretched, but he didn't add anything, walking towards the door again with a cheerful smile. She followed with a sick sensation of relief. He wasn't going to spring news of a marriage to Diana on her, after all, but her relief didn't last long because although the blow had not fallen tonight Diana's presence here must have some meaning and Ferdy might merely be postponing the announcement until what he considered a more suitable time.

Mrs Hammond was hovering in the hall as they came downstairs and Ferdy went to speak to her, smiling. 'Problems, Mrs Hammond?' The housekeeper looked apologetic.

'I'm so sorry for the delay in serving dinner, but the electricity supply seems to be on low power, the oven is taking longer to cook the beef than I'd expected. It won't be long now, though.'

'Never mind, we're in no hurry—I expect the

cold weather has meant a cut in power,' Ferdy
reassured.

Miranda wandered on to the drawing-room
opening the door and pausing with a stiffening
smile as she stared across the room.

Sean and Diana were both standing in front of
the fire; very close together, staring into each
other's eyes in what seemed to Miranda an
intimate fashion, an impression underlined by the
fact that Diana had one hand on Sean's shoulder
the vivid flame of her fingernails startling against
the black of his sweater. As Miranda opened the
door the room was silent, but it vibrated with
whatever had been happening in it before she
appeared, and as her eyes flashed across the room
to catch that frozen little tableau they started and
moved apart to face her. Or, at least, Sean
moved—Diana stayed exactly where she was
posed in mocking self-assurance, lifting the hand
which Sean had shaken off his shoulder to
smooth back her blonde hair, while she glanced
sideways towards Miranda with a satisfied smile.

'Find the presents?' Sean asked coolly, meeting
Miranda's hard stare without blinking. His hair
looked ruffled, as though someone had just run
fingers through it, but it wasn't that that made
Miranda's veins run ice-water. It was the faint
trace of lipstick on his cheek; that shade was not
her own.

'Yes,' she said through her teeth. What had
been going on? Angrily she told herself that she
didn't need to have anyone draw a diagram, did
she? That had been no polite conversation she

had interrupted. Diana's body had been curved blatantly towards Sean, her red-tipped hand stroking his shoulder in a slow, sensual movement which reminded Miranda of a cat kneading a victim with one sheathed paw. Which of them had made the first move? Or did it really matter? Sean hadn't exactly been repelling Diana's advances, perhaps he had even invited them?

Ferdy bustled into the room and Miranda sank back on to the sofa and watched her father unwrapping his presents. At least he seemed genuinely delighted with the hand-made pottery horse and the small watercolour painted by a local artist who they had watched painting in the streets, of a harbour near the villa.

Sean was pouring himself another whisky. Over his shoulder he asked: 'Would you like another sherry, Miranda?' and she heard herself saying quietly: 'No, thank you.' Keep calm, she told herself. Act as if you hadn't noticed a thing. It could mean nothing. Diana might have made an opportunistic pass at Sean out of sheer mischief, it didn't mean he had invited or wanted it.

'I love these subtle colours,' Ferdy said, holding up the little watercolour and staring at it with his head to one side. 'You know my taste, Miranda.'

'She spent ages choosing it,' Sean said with amusement and she felt him looking sideways at her through his black lashes as he sat down beside her.

'Thank you, darling,' Ferdy said, blowing her a kiss.

'I'm glad you like it,' she said as if she hadn't a care in the world, smiling back at him. What if what she had just seen had been no spur of the moment pass but something a good deal more sinister and worrying? Her stomach clenched and as Sean settled close to her, his arm going round the back of her again, she struggled to keep a bright smile on her face.

That was a crazy idea, she wished she hadn't let it creep into her head. After all, hadn't she heard Diana making pretty snide remarks about Sean to her cousin?

Her mind sharply pointed out that Diana could have been lying, might not have wanted anyone— even her cousin—to know that she had a very secret relationship with Sean.

No, that's impossible, she thought quickly, angrily, but her mind would not be quiet. It hadn't even occurred to her to suspect a secret liaison between Diana and Sean, but what if there was one? She had to think this out, she felt her imagination racing like an overheated engine, she must not let this get out of proportion—but what if they had been having a furtive affair for a long time? What if they had planned to keep their love affair hidden while they each openly pursued the future they could never have if they married each other?

She felt a stab of pain and was surprised to find that she had dug her nails into her palms. Why was she letting herself think such things? Sean might be ambitious but she couldn't believe he would stoop to such behaviour; lying, cheating, conspiring. The very idea of him having a furtive affair with Diana while he pretended to ... no, she couldn't bear to consider it. It was too sickening. She could believe it of Diana—she could believe anything of Diana, but she refused to believe Sean capable of it.

Mrs Hammond tapped on the door and came in to say with an apologetic smile: 'Dinner is ready now, sir. I'm so sorry for the delay.'

'It wasn't your fault, Mrs Hammond,' Ferdy said, still holding up the watercolour. 'See what Mrs Hinton has brought me back? Isn't it lovely?'

'Oh, yes, lovely, sir,' Mrs Hammond agreed, eyeing it with what Miranda guessed to be mixed emotions. Mrs Hammond was not artistic; to her the pictures which Ferdy liked to hang on the walls were merely dust traps which made more work for her.

Diana sauntered from the fire, the sway of her body calculated. Miranda shot Sean a rapid look and saw him watching the other woman with an odd little smile playing around his mouth. Her skin went icy with fear and jealousy and a sick dismay. What exactly did that smile mean?

CHAPTER NINE

THE rest of the evening passed, for Miranda, in something of a blur; helped considerably by the number of glasses of wine she was drinking. Normally, she drank very little, and the speed with which she drained each glass soon registered with Sean, whose black brows rose steeply as he watched her finish off yet another glass. She had no idea what she had eaten; food had appeared in front of her and she had idly pushed it around her plate and sent most of it away untouched. She wasn't sure what had been said, either—the two men had done most of the talking. Ferdy was discussing business with Sean whenever she surfaced; filling him in on all the details of what had happened while they were away.

Once Ferdy turned to smile apologetically at her: 'Are we boring you to sleep, Miranda? We shouldn't talk shop over dinner—tell us some more about the island crafts, what else did you buy there?'

She lifted her head in a languid movement, shrugging, murmuring something, and Sean covered for her, quickly.

'She wanted to buy everything she saw but we would never have got back on the plane if she had.'

Miranda lapsed into comforting stupor, staring blankly at the flicker of the candles in the centre of the table. Mrs Hammond had arranged a low trough of spring flowers beside the candles; the fragile scent of primroses and violets drifted across the room, making the howl of the wind and the beating of the snow on the windows seem even more unseasonable. Only yesterday, she had sunbathed on the beach below the villa; the world was full of contradictions, crazy and bewildering contrasts, she felt she understood nothing of what happened around her and she was tired of the doubts and uncertainties beating inside her head. At least the wine was dulling her senses, removing her a little from the pain of watching Sean talk politely to Diana as though they were almost strangers, even as if they were enemies, in fact, wearing civilised masks behind which other feelings lurked. If she had not opened that door and seen them staring at each other, Miranda might have been deceived by the occasional sting in Diana's voice, the cold mockery of Sean's fleeting smile in reply. She might have thought, as they undoubtedly intended her to think, that they disliked each other but were hiding it.

As she served their coffee, Mrs Hammond said cheerfully: 'The snow has stopped at last and the wind's dropping. Let's hope we'll have some better weather tomorrow.'

Sean wandered over to the drawing-room windows and pulled back the curtains to stare at the sky which glittered with a frosty moonlight.

'I'm going to have a difficult drive back,' Diana said, ruefully smiling at Ferdy, her lashes fluttering. 'I'd better leave in a minute.'

'Stay the night,' he said at once, as she had meant him to, but she pretended to hesitate.

'Oh, I couldn't put you to that trouble!' she said, waiting to be persuaded.

Sean turned with a dry smile. 'I'll drive you back, in the estate car—that can cope with these road conditions without any trouble. Drink your coffee and we'll be on our way.'

Miranda stiffened; jealousy stabbing inside her, images of them together, alone, making love, laughing at her, the pictures blurring together with a tormented rush.

'You don't want to go out again tonight,' Ferdy said, looking startled and frowning. 'There's no need for it—Diana can stay here, it's much more sensible. Good heavens, there is plenty of room— Mrs Hammond can make up the bed in the room Miranda used to have.'

Sean sauntered back coolly. 'It won't take me long to drive Diana home and I could do with some fresh air.'

'I don't want to be a nuisance,' Diana said quickly. 'I couldn't take you out on your first night home, Miranda would never forgive me.' She gave an unconvincing laugh, her eyes flicking to Miranda, inviting her to join in the discussion, but Miranda declined, looking away blankly at the fire. The orange flames leapt up the chimney, tiny red sparks flung off from them with a crackle. She did not want Diana sleeping under the same roof as herself, but she did not want Sean driving away with her, either. She was puzzled by Sean's insistence and Diana's reluctance; what exactly was behind their tug of war? Whatever was really going on, though, she saw no point in trying to intervene, she refused to admit she cared one way or the other.

'Miranda is very sleepy,' Sean said, leaning down to stroke a stray strand of dark brown hair from her cheek, a display of loving concern she was tempted to reject angrily but which with Ferdy and Diana watching, she accepted without a word. 'Why don't you go up to bed darling? You're half asleep in that chair. It won't take me more than half an hour to drive Diana to her flat and get back here.'

'Maybe I will,' she said, getting up, her eyes heavy. She kissed Ferdy lightly, gave Diana a brief look and a terse: 'Good night,' and let Sean steer her to the door, his arm around her. He opened the door and she silently suffered his kiss on her hair before walking away without a backward look.

She bolted the bedroom door and got undressed, refusing to think refusing to feel. Climbing into the big double bed she put out the light and let sleep wash over her; a heavy, wine-induced sleep without dreams, or none that she remembered when she woke up. She lay for a while, staring at the dark ceiling, slowly coming back to awareness of a number of things—firstly, that she had a violent headache, and then in quick succession that her mouth was as dry as a kiln, her body damp with the perspiration of that heavy sleep, her eyes hot and her mind in turmoil. Lifting her head to look at the clock she

winced at the stab of pain the movement sent
through her. It was almost five in the morning,
she discovered. The birds hadn't yet begun to
sing. The house was silent—and she was still
alone.

She sat up very carefully, clutching her
forehead, swung off the bed and switched on the
light, blinking as the brightness assailed her eyes.
She needed some aspirin. Groping her way into
the bathroom she hunted in the cupboard, but
Mrs Hammond hadn't thought of stocking it with
anything but a selection of bath salts and soap
and talcs, shampoo and bubble bath, conditioner
and body oil. Miranda impatiently pushed aside
all the cans and bottles and packets, groaning as
her head throbbed. In the mirror lining the wall
above the bath she saw her face, white and
strained, her dark blue eyes reflecting pain.

Had Sean ever come back from driving Diana
home? Had he spent the night with her? Ferdy
would most probably have gone to bed when
Sean and Diana left. Her father went to bed quite
early, especially when he was going to work next
day. Who would have known whether Sean came
back right away, or whether he stayed for hours?

'Oh, damn,' she muttered, turning away from
the cupboard. She would have to go down to the
kitchen to look for a painkiller. She pulled a loose
silk robe over her nightie and went to the
bedroom door. When it didn't move as she
tugged the handle she stared impatiently. Now
what was wrong? She tugged again, then
remembered bolting the door before she got

undressed. She slid back the bolt and crept down the corridor, down the stairs, listening to the silence in the house. Where was Sean? Had he tried her door and retreated? Or hadn't he come back at all?

The kitchen lay at the far back of the house. It was full of a peculiar snowy light; the grey dawn given a new colour by reflecting off the snow covering the whole garden. She found some pills almost immediately, took two of them with a glass of cold water and stood at the kitchen window staring out at the trees in their crystalline glitter; bare branches frozen in a wrapping of snow which sparkled as the light fell on it.

Turning away with a sigh she got some milk out of the fridge and heated it in a saucepan; she might as well take some chocolate back to bed with her, it wasn't going to be easy to get back to sleep even now that her headache was slackening a little as the pills began to work.

As she crept through the hall again five minutes later she thought she heard a board creak somewhere and stiffened, listening intently, but there was no further sound so she went softly up to the bedroom.

She was halfway across the carpet before she saw Sean. She almost dropped the cup; it shook in her grip and drops of hot chocolate splashed out on her hand, making her gasp. 'Damn!' She put the cup down on the bedside table, grabbed a tissue from an open box and dried her hand, ignoring Sean as he rose from the chair by the curtained window.

'I've just spent the night downstairs in a chair,' he grated, his voice kept low but the timbre of it harsh enough to make her nerves jump. 'Don't ever bolt a door against me again or . . .'

'Or what?' she asked, turning to face him, her chin lifted belligerently, and her voice charged with all the bitterness and contempt she felt. 'You don't frighten me!'

His eyes narrowed, his tanned skin drawn tightly over his cheekbones and his mouth compressed with rage. He was fully dressed, wearing the same black sweater and grey pants he had worn last night, his hair ruffled and a dark shadow roughening his jaw where he needed to shave. He looked menacing and as he took a step towards her she was tempted to run, but faced it out. They weren't alone any more; she only had to scream and her father would come running to find out what on earth was happening to her.

'Why did you bolt that door?' he demanded.

'I thought you'd be staying at Diana's,' she told him coolly, and his eyes suddenly widened in wary surprise.

'What did you say?'

'You heard me.'

'I heard the words, but what did they mean?' he asked slowly, and she gave an indifferent shrug.

'I'm not as stupid as you think.'

Sean's gaze probed her face in silence for so long that her nerves shrieked in protest, then he said drily: 'You're crazy, not stupid. What are you accusing me of now? Making a pass at Diana? I'd rather tangle with a cobra. I spent a good hour straightening your father out about her this evening; it was time someone put him wise about her schemes and ambitions. I don't know what bee you've got in your bonnet, but I'm getting pretty tired of being accused of every crime under the sun on no evidence other that the latest twist of your suspicious little mind.'

'No evidence?' she said bitterly. 'What about the lipstick on your face? She kissed you while I was upstairs with my father and don't deny it because you're not going to convince me I didn't see it.'

He stared at her, his lips twisting in a wry smile. 'My God, you've got eyes like gimlets. Yes, she kissed me—it was a last ditch attempt to stop me talking to Ferdy. She made me an offer I had no problem refusing.'

Miranda's head was dizzy with a mixture of uncertainty and angry hope. Had she been completely off the track after all? There was something reassuring in the sardonic impatience in his eyes; he didn't show any sign of guilt or alarm. Her legs felt weak, she sat down suddenly on the bed.

'You talked to my father about her?'

'I thought it was time somebody did. I wasn't sure how he felt about her, so I tackled him warily at first, testing the ground, but eventually I realised that I wouldn't be breaking Ferdy's heart by disillusioning him, so I told him what you'd overheard and all about the chat I had with Diana while you and your father were up here looking for the presents.'

'You told her I'd overheard her?' Miranda flushed. She hadn't wanted Diana to know she had been eavesdropping. It was humiliating enough to have heard all that without Diana knowing that she had been listening like a parlour maid at a keyhole.

Sean gave an impatient sigh. 'Of course not! I merely told her politely that when I became managing director I would promote my present secretary along with me, and that Diana ought to start looking for another job.'

Miranda drew a sharp breath. 'What did she say?'

He smiled drily. 'What do you think? That she worked for Ferdy, not me, and that she would talk to him about what I'd said. I told her she could talk to him—but first I'd be telling him all about the chat she had had with her cousin the night before the wedding. While she was still reeling from the shock of that, I added that she needn't bother to deny it because I had a witness who could repeat everything she had said.'

Miranda stared at him, eyes wide open. 'She asked who it was, of course?'

Sean sat down a few feet away from her, leaning back on his elbows while he grinned at her. 'She should have done—but being a woman, she didn't. She jumped to conclusions instead, and made some very nasty remarks about her cousin Paul. For some reason she at once suspected that he had sold the information to me because he didn't trust Diana to get him a promotion he wanted. When she had stopped

:alling him names she changed her tune, said he
vas lying, none of it was true, but she wasn't
:onvincing even to herself. She'd lost her head
or a minute and she knew it. For a woman like
Diana to lose her head publicly was humiliating.
She looked at me as if she would have liked to
tick a knife in me.'

Miranda didn't say anything, but she had often
elt that way herself, especially lately, and her
eyes held a frosty sparkle which Sean watched
quizzically as if reading her mind.

'So when did she kiss you?' she asked coldly.

'A minute before you came in,' he said. 'I
vouldn't be surprised if she hadn't heard your
voice and decided to kill two birds with one
tone. She stopped snarling at me and made a
sudden pass, saying something about couldn't we
:ome to a very private arrangement, and, in case I
didn't get her drift, kissed me. She meant to kiss
ny mouth but I drew back and said, "No deal,
Diana." Then you came in.'

'I knew something had been going on!'

'And jumped to a few conclusions of your
own?' he drawled. 'So that's why you drank
yourself under the table.'

'I did not!'

'Not literally, maybe, but I began to wonder
how you would make it upstairs. I thought I
night have to carry you.'

Flushed, she said crossly: 'I drank a few glasses
of wine! Don't make such a big deal of it.'

'If I hadn't steered you to the door you
wouldn't have found it.'

'I was tired!'

He laughed mockingly. 'You were jealous.'

'I was not!' Her face burning, she stammered 'Jealous? Don't be funny! Over you? I couldn' care less what you . . .'

'Diana's parting arrow found its target, didn' it?' he drawled, his mouth derisive. 'That's partl why she kissed me—she wanted you to see, sh wanted to make trouble between us, the woman i pure poison.' He shifted, turning sideways an patting the double bed. 'I thought it was this tha was bothering you.'

Her flush became hectic and she looked down

'Which just goes to show how dangerous it i to think you can read someone else's mind,' Sea said.

'Doesn't it,' Miranda muttered. She tried s often to read his—without success.

'Especially one like yours! I had no idea femal thinking was so tortuous and irrational,' Sea said with a crooked smile.

Miranda let that pass. She had had almost a much trouble understanding her own mind as sh had in trying to read his—during the past tw weeks she had discovered things about hersel which she had not suspected. In struggling t uncover the real man behind Sean's bewilderin mask she had been brought face to face with th difference between the surface and the interio life of every individual. If she couldn't eve understand herself half the time, how could sh hope to understand anyone else? In learning tha she had taken a huge stride towards a maturit

he had blithely believed hers already. Perhaps
ou were never really an adult until you realised
ow little you knew of yourself or anyone else.

'What did Ferdy say when you told him?' she
sked and Sean leaned back, his supple body
ompletely relaxed, smiling ironically.

'That's another maddening female trick! When
ou're backed into a corner, you wriggle out of it
y changing the subject,' he observed, but went
n coolly: 'He wasn't as astounded as you might
ave expected. I told him the whole story when I
ot back from driving Diana home. I was
determined not to let her stay here tonight, I
vanted a chance to talk to Ferdy before she got to
im. If he was hooked on her, there wouldn't
ave been much we could do except warn him.
He's a grown man with a mind of his own;
owever much of a bitch she is, he might still
ave wanted her.'

Miranda frowned and he gave her a dry look.
Face it, Miranda—your father's a man like
nybody else and Diana is a very sexy female.
Some men go for her type. I didn't know if Ferdy
vas one of them, but I soon realised that he was
n two minds about her. He finds her physically
ttractive and he admires her brains—but he had
qualms of doubt. Diana hadn't been about to get
proposal. Apparently he had sounded you out
nd you'd made it clear that you didn't like her.'
Sean looked through his lashes at Miranda,
miling. 'You needn't have worried, you see. You
lways had the power to put a stop to Diana's
ittle game. Nobody in this world matters as

much to Ferdy as you do. Once he knew yo
weren't in favour of Diana, she had had it.'

'I almost feel sorry for her,' Miranda said, fac
sombre.

Sean laughed shortly. 'Don't be. Diana is he
own worst enemy, you know. She is so bus
being contemptuous of the motives of everyon
around her that she never really understands th
people she's dealing with. Cynicism may b
protective but it's also destructive when it take
no account of human nature. Ferdy may be a
tough as shoe leather when he's doing busines
but he's a family man under that, and h
instincts warned him that Diana wasn't th
home-making kind. Ferdy has a warm heart an
he needs a woman who can make him happy
Sean gave her a sardonic look. 'I wonder ho
well you know your father, either? You can
know him well, or you'd have confided in hi
instead of running off to pour out your trouble
to Clare Holm, that night. How do you think h
built up a company as big as ours without a ver
shrewd idea of what made human beings tick?'

'You said yourself that business is one thing—
and emotions are something else. I was to
disturbed to know what to think after I'd overhear
Diana and her cousin. I needed to get away to think

'You've done too much thinking and n
enough feeling,' Sean said dangerously, his bod
sliding along the bed.

Miranda moved hurriedly back from hir
saying urgently: 'Then Diana will be leaving th
company?'

He nodded, his eyes gleaming. 'I've no doubt he'll demand a hefty redundancy cheque but Ferdy won't quibble with her over that. She's a clever lady; she'll get a job as good.'

'You must be tired if you've sat up all night,' Miranda said quickly. 'Why don't you get some sleep now? It's gone six but I'll make sure you aren't disturbed.'

He shot out a hand as she got up and she felt the firm fingers tighten around her wrist with a stab of alarm.

'It's you who's afraid of being disturbed,' he murmured softly, pulling her back down towards him. 'Did you bolt that door again?'

She struggled against the strong hands compelling her closer. 'Yes, but . . .'

'Good,' Sean said, tilting her backwards on the bed and arching over her, the weight of his body pinioning her on the rumpled sheets. 'I don't want any interruptions for the next few hours. We have a lot of lost time to catch up on . . .'

She held him away, her hands flattened on his shoulders, her flush hectic. 'Sean, I can't live with a man who doesn't love me. You said I didn't understand Ferdy, that he needed a woman who would make him happy—well, I understand only too well. That's what I need, too, a man who loves me, not one who married me because he thought I'd make a suitable wife or bring him a successful company.'

Sean's eyes held an angry brilliance. 'I told you that we were arguing over the meanings of words, but you wouldn't listen. We could argue over the

definition of love all night and get nowhere, but
you stop keeping me at arm's length for just a
hour, we could abandon theory and start findin
out about each other with some more bas
practice.'

'And I told you that sex isn't all there is
love!' she threw back, the throb in her hea
returning.

'That isn't all I want from you but it's
damned sight easier to understand than word
Half the time you mean one thing and I mea
another. You have a tendency to jump
conclusions, you get emotional over somethin
you've dreamed up in your own head, the wa
you did because you sensed that Diana and
hadn't just been talking about the weather whi
we were alone. If you'd really looked at he
you'd have seen an angry, shaken woman, but n
You had her down in your book as a *femm
fatale*, so you decided that I'd made a pass at he
You couldn't have been more wrong.'

'I wasn't wrong in suspecting that you an
Ferdy planned our marriage before such an ide
ever entered my head!'

Sean sighed, his mouth hard. 'Your fathe
nudged me into dating you—that's true. It's ju
as true that there was never a moment when
stopped in my tracks, saying: I'm in love wit
Miranda! I thought you were pretty and I aske
you out. We seemed to get on well, the more
saw of you the more I enjoyed your compan
But I still didn't tell myself that I was madly i
love with you. That's not the way my min

works. I told you before—I don't even know exactly what people mean when they say they're in love. If there are magical signs, I never noticed them. I noticed what lovely eyes you have. I noticed that you look your best in blue. I noticed that you have soft skin I like touching and that your body moves gracefully. There was quite a lot about you that I noticed over the weeks and, apart from the fact that you're prone to get crazy ideas, I liked everything I noticed.'

She lay very still, listening to him and frustratedly wishing she could shake something more comforting out of him.

'I don't like analysing my emotions,' he said with a sudden twist of the mouth which had a faintly sulky air.

'Do you have any?' she asked bitterly and got an impatient look.

'What do you want me to say? Of course I have emotions; I distrust the sort of violent reaction you seem to think betrays emotion, Miranda. I didn't enjoy being jealous of the guy you fished out of the sea but I couldn't reason myself out of it because I knew damned well that you were in such a childish mood that you might encourage him just to get your own back on me.'

She looked down, half smiling. 'Who, me?'

'Yes, you,' he said. 'Don't look innocent, you don't fool me—you wanted to make me jealous.'

'Don't be ridiculous. Now who's imagining things?' she said, her dark blue eyes very bright behind their curtain of lashes.

'Woman have a very primitive streak,' Sean

muttered, his mouth sardonic. 'Like tigers they enjoy a kill and they are difficult to civilise.'

Miranda bristled, her eyes lifting: 'Thanks! If you're so civilised how come you were jealous of poor Marty Knox? He was grateful to me for saving his life and you treated him like Public Enemy Number One.'

'I was thinking emotionally—you keep claiming that that's what you want me to do! Now you're complaining when I do it.'

She watched him, a pulse beating fast at the base of her throat. 'How could you think emotionally if you don't love me?'

Sean's dark eyes glinted. 'I didn't say I didn't love you—I never said that. I said I wasn't "in love", I said I didn't know what that meant and I still don't. I don't feel I'm walking on air when I see you or hear bells ring when you speak or any of that romantic rubbish.'

Miranda lay back on the bed, her hands moving along his shoulders and around his neck very slowly. Sean watched her, face intent. She looked at him through her lashes, smiling, and saw his throat move convulsively. Miranda's fingers stroked his nape and Sean looked at her mouth, his lids hooding his eyes.

'I want you,' he whispered urgently. 'You don't know how much. You've been driving me crazy.'

'But you're not in love with me,' she mocked softly, and felt his restless movement, the frustrated tension in his body.

'Call it what you like,' he groaned, his hands

reaching for her again, and moving over the silken warmth of her body with shaky urgency. 'Stop saying no, Miranda, let me love you. I can't go on like this; the suspense is killing me. I married you because I wanted you as my wife; I wanted you in my bed and in my home, I wanted to be with you every day of my life. I love watching you, whatever you're doing, you fascinate me, I'm never bored when I'm with you.' His eyes closed and he buried his flushed face against her throat, kissing it passionately. Miranda was very still, happiness glowing in her dark blue eyes as she listened. The rough, unsteady voice was so convincing and Sean might not call the way he felt being in love but that was what Miranda called it.

'I find it very hard to talk about things like that,' he muttered into her skin, his hands doing violent things to her pulse rate. 'It makes me feel stupid, exposed . . .'

'Vulnerable?' she whispered, stroking the ruffled mass of dark hair, and he made an inaudible sound which could have meant anything. Sean couldn't even bring himself to admit that he found vulnerability worrying. He couldn't admit he was in love or needed anyone, perhaps because for so long he had trained himself to be strong and responsible, so that he could take care of Declan and any circumstances he was forced to meet. Sean had a strong idea of masculinity and responsibility: weakness disturbed him, threatened the strength he felt he should have. An ordinary human need for love might betray him;

she saw now that to Sean love was like a flaw, a crack in his defences against the world, he was almost ashamed of it, he was certainly afraid of his own feelings.

With another flash of insight she saw that it had been his male strength which she had always found so attractive. What did she, herself, want of love? Hadn't her father's constant watchful care of her given her a deeply imprinted image of the man she needed to make her happy? Sean had been that man because he was more like her father than any man she had yet met and she had been confused by that, but her instincts had been wiser than herself, recognising the distinction between those two relationships and needing to break past the outer strength to find the vulnerable human being behind it. She and Sean had been locked in a conflict between their two deepest needs. Sean had wanted to conceal his weakness, she had needed to be shown it.

She looked at him passionately, sliding a hand down his back, her body arching towards him. 'I love you,' she said huskily, deliberately, and felt his body stiffen.

His lips hunted along her cheek, found her mouth, his arms moved under her and lifted her closer, pressed tightly and possessively along the length of his body while they kissed.

Minutes later she heard Sean mutter something, muffled, reluctant. She didn't hear the actual words, but she felt them; not simply moving against her mouth but right through her whole body. She had waited a long, long time to hear Sean say: 'I love you,' with such depth and need, she was weak with happiness as she realised he had said it at last, but his sensual urgency gave her no time to think about it, his hands moving with erotic demands exploring the undefended territory of her body.

'Miranda?' he groaned with a last hoarse uncertainty before he took her, as if he still expected resistance, and her body arched to meet his.

The bride had stopped saying no.

No one Can Resist . . .

HARLEQUIN
REGENCY ROMANCES

Regency romances take you back to a time when men fought for their ladies' honor and passions—a time when heroines had to choose between love and duty . . . with love always the winner!

Enjoy these three authentic novels of love and romance set in one of the most colorful periods of England's history.

Lady Alicia's Secret by Rachel Cosgrove Payes

She had to keep her true identity hidden—at least until she was convinced of his love!

Deception So Agreeable by Mary Butler

She reacted with outrage to his false proposal of marriage, then nearly regretted her decision.

The Country Gentleman by Dinah Dean

She refused to believe the rumors about him— certainly until they could be confirmed or denied!

Everyone Loves . . .

HARLEQUIN GOTHIC ROMANCES

A young woman lured to an isolated estate far from help and civilization . . . a man, lonely, tortured by a centuries' old commitment . . . and a sinister force threatening them both and their newfound love . . .

Read these three superb novels of romance and suspense . . . as timeless as love and as filled with the unexpected as tomorrow!

Return To Shadow Creek by Helen B. Hicks

She returned to the place of her birth—only to discover a sinister plot lurking in wait for her. . . .

Shadows Over Briarcliff by Marilyn Ross

Her visit vividly brought back the unhappy past—and with it an unknown evil presence. . . .

The Blue House by Dolores Holliday

She had no control over the evil forces that were driving her to the brink of madness. . . .

Take 4 novels and a surprise gift FREE